DEAD BAIT 2

SEVERED PRESS

INTRODUCTION

By J Gilliam Martin

Myself, I have set foot in the ocean but a handful of times. I have submerged myself in over-head depth only once. It was a snorkeling trip around a reef off the coast of the Bahamas. My fascination of the sea and fair share of rum and punch fueled my courage enough to ignore the long list of fears I brought with me aboard that boat.

I was more than happy to explore once in the water, comforted by my inebriation and the swarm of other people also participating. I remained close to the surface, keeping the air within reach during most of my dive. When I learned of the possibility of an octopus hiding under a crevice below, I submerged a couple of times to investigate, having always wanted to see one of these creatures up close. Though I had become more relaxed in the environment since talk of the trip that morning, I still couldn't help feeling like a sitting duck.

The reef was beautiful and well lit. The water was a crystal clear blue, and my visits to the surface were becoming less frequent. However, every time I considered my surroundings and looked about, I could not see more than six feet off in the distance. My heart rate would quicken whenever I looked anywhere away but the reef itself, which was not on the coast at all, mind you, but sort of an underwater island in what I remember being at least a half-mile from land. In any kind of emergency I had one option: get to the boat. Around the time I had nearly left all my fears behind and lost track of the boat's location, I spotted a considerably large silhouette in my peripheral. I gasped a few bubbles and stilled myself as best I could, then stared in its direction.

If you have ever seen a barracuda face to face, you know that they are ugly as all hell and heavily armed with teeth. One of these visual abominations had taken an interest in me on my dive. He stayed there, just barely visible in the water's fog, and he was watching me.

When you spot a wild animal on land, you either observe it, or you shoot it. We are fascinated by the sight of them. People go to zoos to just to look at the various species, and in nature they will stare in wonder as a creature runs by on its normal routine. In the woods, the animals are scared of us and they will most often run away.

This was not the case with this fish. He was watching me, and I was suffering fear.

I swam around the reef to put a gap between us and get bearings on the boat. My swimming speed and skill was enhanced by the moment of panic that this aquatic, living chainsaw might be on my tail. I harbored no knowledge of these particular fish. I had never seen one or even bothered to read about one, and had no idea whether or not a barracuda had a history of attacking people, I just assumed so. With the general fear I brought to the table, he might as well have been a giant, genetically engineered, prehistoric zombie-shark, ready to take my fate into his mouth.

Sure enough around the other side of the reef, that same six feet away, he had followed. His little black eyes were still fixed on me, just beyond the point where my vision was blurred by the murk of the water.

I noticed that in my attempt to evade its gaze, I had swam to an area of the reef everyone else had finished exploring, and was all alone. Alone, but with this goddamn monster, who surely would come for a taste of my flesh at any moment.

I charged him, yelling underwater. My fear had taken control of my body and used its natural human-defense (a pathetic and useless one, proven so throughout time) of screaming obscenities and shaking fists.

The barracuda was not bothered, he didn't even move.

Fuck that. I fled as fast as those flippers would take me to the nearest group of swimmers and reported my would-be murderer, but no one was interested. They laughed at me, if anything. After my complaining and show of paranoia during the boat ride out to our diving spot, I could have been yelling, "Shark!", and everyone would have shook their heads at me in pity.

Maybe they were right. It was just a fish, after all, probably not quite my size and based on my father's teachings in my youth, probably just as interested and/or scared of me as I was of him.

Then I am approached by my youngest brother, one of the most fearless beings I have ever met. He was all amped up, breathing heavy and talking fast. I don't get to mention my tormenter before he tells me he has been swimming through the reef rather than around it. Finding holes and tunnels just big enough for his tiny frame, he was seeing parts of this area I would never imagine.

He goes on, talking of one of his tunnels with the water level uneven, and sometimes air would go through it. Drunk with adrenaline, he explains to me how I could catch it just right and a wave would carry you through the hole, and it is amazing. But his story ends for me when he explains that his last time through he caught the wave wrong and it lifted him too soon. He smashed up his back and thought for a minute he might not make it to the other end, but was here panting from the thrill of survival to tell me all about it.

At this moment the only thing I could think of was his back. I spun him around in the water to see a large scrape from his shoulder-blade down to the crack of his ass, seeping blood into the water behind him.

He was bleeding into the fucking ocean. This was the end of the snorkeling adventure for me. I promptly swam back to the boat, climbed aboard and equipped myself with rum, never so glad to have a solid surface beneath my feet and a cold drink in my hand.

And as I stood there on the back of the boat as everyone still swam around the reef, including my baited brother, I swear a barracuda was circling the boat.

My thing with water, particularly the sea, is that you don't know what's down there. It's not really any different than being afraid of the dark, though it seems far more reasonable to me. There is much more water than land on this planet, and we are still exploring it. They find new or evolved species regularly.

I think there is a good amount of helplessness involved in aquaphobia as well. Our bodies were not made for traversing waters. We have no gills, webbing, or fins to assist us. Swallow too much water and you fail to float.

Imagine yourself treading water in the middle of the ocean. Look below you. You cannot see a thing, not even your own hands. Now imagine how many things can see you.

No matter the body of water, you can only see so far. This book should give you a few more things to be concerned with. Concerned that just below your visibility, in the murk or depths of the water, lies something to which you are an intruder, and in the worlds of Dead Bait, that makes you a target.

www.jgilliammartin.com

CONTENTS

CAPTAIN FONTAINE AND THE MAN EATER

Raleigh Dugal

Captain Fontaine possessed a certain rudimentary madness not commonly found in thirty-five year old men. His affliction was the sort usually reserved for middle-aged women who may suddenly find themselves amid a dreary marriage that has born shockingly ugly children, dwelling in a frostbitten state with fickle, nearly violent weather, and working at a fancy law office for a finely dressed man on the cusp of old age with bad taste in shoes and good taste in wine. At this particular law office, the woman could compare the dark mahogany desks and satin chairs with her drab plaid couch and particle board entertainment center, perhaps imbibing herself with a greater madness and resolve to smother those ugly children with love, let their lives become her own, and live until expiration under the thumb of an extreme infatuation with the monotonous persistence of her nuclear family.

Unfortunately for Fontaine, this was exactly the situation in which his wife found herself after five years of cold dinners and waiting with their whining brood for him to return to shore. However, unlike her husband, she possessed the cool calculation of a Bengal tiger waiting in a bamboo forest and when the time was right, pounced and killed their marriage, picking their relationship clean as the bones of an antelope. Had *she* been the spouse who possessed this specific madness, there is no doubt she would have remained in their white house with the square rows of hedges at the end of Apple Blossom Road, dressing her not one but two pugs in ugly little sweaters and feeding the three children spoonfuls of mashed food as they dropped it on their clothing, all while humming maniacally and sashaying about the linoleum-floored kitchen.

No, it was her luck that all that particular madness resided in Fontaine and so when she departed quickly, leaving a scattered wake of bibs and pacifiers and frilly lingerie in the driveway, he remained.

His scant hair flitted in the breeze off the ocean, the only mistress he had ever known. At the end of the driveway he stopped following her, put his pathetic, melodramatic hand down which had been reaching forward as if to hold on. His madness took over and denied him the ability to believe she did not want to live there with him anymore and if he were to step across the cracks in the pavement that led into the road he was sure the world would crumble.

Her name had been Galadriel and she was pretty, but not beautiful, a washed-out blonde who froze in the winter like crystallized straw and burnt salmon-pink in the short summer months. They'd first met at a dance on the common in Onset Beach when they were seventeen. Fontaine told her that her name sounded like a mermaid's as he felt her breath on his neck beneath the gazebo, slow dancing two feet apart.

But that had been almost twenty years ago, long before her hatred for him and their life and his knowledge that her name had, in fact, been lifted from a character in Lord of the Rings.

Now, instead of stolen gazebo kisses they had children. Pale, membranous creatures of varying ages spaced evenly apart by a year or so, none of them past the age of four. They burbled and cooed silly nonsense words at him, the oldest crying for mama. Not so unlike the strange fish he pulled from the ocean, gasping greedily at the air and pulling nothing but hot, vacant breaths that slowly killed them, the children became the last bastion of real, confirmed love between Fontaine and his wife. He hugged and cuddled them, smiled over them, fed them impromptu bachelor meals like hot dog stew and mashed up cheeseburgers. Finally his mother arrived at the house. She stood in the doorway looking fearfully at the monsters on the couch, lined up like bowling pins.

"I'll watch them as long as you two need to sort things out," his mother offered with just a hint of hesitation, knowing there'd be no sorting out. They packed them, wrapped them in coats and scarves like tuna steaks in wax paper. The four of them, grandmother and grandchildren, trundled north toward Avon and posh suburbs where class could offer them advantages no matter how freakish they may be.

The white house with the square hedges on Apple Blossom Road slowly fell away. Dishes crawled out of the sink and slunk across the countertop until it was impossible to add any more, and a thick skin of crumbs and dried sauces covered them. It seemed a giant, decaying animal with a porcelain skeleton had lay down and died beneath the faucet. Fontaine's bed, forever rumpled, mattress skewed half off the box spring, became a vortex of discolored undershirts and stained pajamas and paint-spattered jeans and later, Chinese take-out and pizza boxes and newspaper classifieds. In the bathroom, the medicine cabinet mirror cracked from the molding, stuffed with pictures of the hideous children and Galadriel, all in which she looked bored and the children looked hungry. Cigarette burns no one would ever care about pocked the surface of the vanity, the rugs, the countertops, like craters in the moon.

And yet, despite the foul detritus accumulated by the sorrow of one man, the house maintained the scent of emptiness, the barren, musty, lack of smell a place possesses when its soul has been stripped.

The home, however, no matter how great a nexus of self-pity it became, was not a clear representation of how Fontaine had soldiered on with his life. To the contrary, he rose heartily like a sodden phoenix every morning at four, out of the garbage pit he slept in, over the scattered socks and underpants in the stairwell, and made himself two English muffins for breakfast and packed a turkey sandwich on rye bread for lunch, which he usually fed to the gulls. When he left for work he left the door unlocked, should Galadriel return.

That silent insanity, the particular madness, had made itself known to Fontaine. He wondered at it daily as he readied the chum on board, grinding junk fish into a soupy puree of guts and meat broth and stirring it evenly with a steel scoop. He was not alone very often. Divorce forced him to work non-stop, so he spent great lengths of time on the bleak ocean with strangers. They were laughing, happy strangers, lots of fathers and sons (his own father had drowned when Fontaine was two, leaving him with memories of half-finished cigarettes and the sound of the lawn mower running, but nothing of the man himself), sometimes moms too, with little daughters in pigtails that made faces at the smell of the fish, and the rare grandmother or aunt who mostly refused to venture down from the air conditioned cockpit. But mostly he kept company with men, bachelor parties and graduation parties and the like, making his madness all the more evident. Domestic longing pitter-pattered within what should have been stone-cold fisherman's blood pumped from some titanic crack in the floor of his abysmal heart.

In reality, Fontaine was no real fisherman. He was a showman, a charter captain, sure. But for him the ocean was a wet, colorless world, bright and harsh or flat and dull, but a thing that resisted personification, as so many people loved to grant it. The ocean was an alien world, an atmosphere. For Fontaine there was nothing human about the ocean at all, only cold depth and mystery, both of which had become so real for him they held little fascination.

Captain Fontaine was wiry and hard, like a spring uncoiled and straightened. His tanned, leathery skin was the color and texture of expensive luggage. A sparse beard clung to his face as if the wind had for years been trying to pry it away and had mostly succeeded. Once blue, his eyes were now faded silver from the constant sun. They never fixed directly on an object, but rather digested everything together in a panorama, the way he'd digest a distant horizon.

Returning home from those horizons, having torn his turkey sandwich to shreds and tossed it to the gulls, he'd be hungry. Then he took his dinner at Hooters.

The restaurant was hardly distinguishable from its exterior, situated in an old white colonial two blocks off the main drag. The building had been a sailors' tavern that failed as the little shops that sold pink flip-flops and beach balls sprung up. The only thing that betrayed the building's nature was its sign, hung high toward the peak of the roof, small and square in accordance with Cape Cod's infamous zoning ordinances that restrict every Dunkin Donuts and CVS and any other establishment in town to four-by-four rectangular signage in order to *maintain the suitable level of quaintness*. Fontaine wondered if quaintness ceased to be *quaint* when it had to be forced.

On dreary March evenings, just before the work season started, Fontaine ambled along Main Street, mind blank, and entered beneath the gaudy orange sign. The glowing owl with breast-shaped eyes stared away at the horizon, like him.

There, Fontaine subsided entirely on Buffalo wings or bacon cheeseburgers with jalapeno cheese, reveling in the fact that the cows and chickens had once lived on solid ground, ingesting the kinetic relationship their feet had had with planet earth. Seafood had lost its appeal to him long ago, as a child, when he'd learnt the strangeness of the ocean and the dark, inhuman wrath of its moods and denizens. Its creatures were not for eating. They were spiny, shining mouths and eyes and lips, sums of parts without consciousness or souls. Once when he was seven, on the same beach where he met Galadriel, a boy named Tony Barrett plucked a horseshoe crab from the water and dangled it by the tail in front of Fontaine's nose, all shell and legs and motion.

"Why ain't you screamin'?" the older boy demanded.

"Gimme something to scream about," young Fontaine replied, spindly and tan even then.

So Tony Barrett pinned Fontaine to the sand and let the crab crawl along his back, through his hair. He didn't utter a sound. When Tony Barrett let him up, he picked up the crab himself and put it back in the water.

It was important to Fontaine to differentiate what he felt for the ocean from fear or hate. It was certainly not love, but it wasn't those other things, either. Perhaps, deep down under the blanket of his madness, the emotion was a longing to be as cold and numb and distant as a Moray eel or a sea urchin, a kind of resentment of their detachment. Or it might have been a sad, ironic respect for creatures so instinctual they might later in life consume their own offspring and never know a thing about it.

Regulars at Hooters joked that spicy food kept the Captain alive, he worked so damn much. Others said it wasn't the spicy food, but the swollen, dangling breasts of the waitresses swaying above round hips poured into bright orange daisy dukes.

But Fontaine harbored no desire for the girls. Many of his neighbors, wives of local politicians or seasonal spinsters who became permanent out of romanticism for the Cape's quiet festivity long ago, called him a slimy deadbeat. Some even gossiped that his wife and children were at the bottom of the canal (no one knew the exact details of his wife's absence, not even his mother knew the story in its entirety). Truth was that Fontaine went to Hooter's for business.

A dependable tide of tourists roared through the restaurant each spring. Some were snotty Ivy League college kids, clad in torn corduroys and tight t-shirts, others just scummy lawyers in blue pinstripes. The occasional old-money blueblood straggled in for kicks every now and then sporting khaki shorts, a sweater around his neck and a charitable twinkle in his eye, as if he breathed dollar bills, which was never far from the truth.

These men were a catch more valuable than Fontaine could ever harvest in the ocean. Usually he'd buy them a beer, chat about Hyannis and ask if they'd checked out the British Beer Co. or Tim's Books. To a lawyer he'd bemoan the sorry state of the judicial system or with the students, the sorry state of anything, and with the bluebloods, the big fish, how damn-spanking wonderful the world could be. Somehow by the end of the conversation someone was using his card as a coaster or, more often, writing one of the waitress' numbers on the back. Next morning he'd be dehydrated and overbooked and spend the day calling parties and rearranging his schedule while drinking Gatorade and swallowing Aleve by the handful.

Bachelor parties, birthday parties, weddings, bar mitzvahs; every one of them and more had boarded the *Glory Hound*. Once, an old Pole from Danvers wheeled himself onto the boat, alone, wheezing like a broken vacuum cleaner, half-crazy with cancer meds and marijuana, raving about hunting for Moby Dick. Fontaine called an old lawyer client and prepared the necessary paperwork in case the Polak croaked on the boat. They trolled for three days and caught nothing but colds and sunburns. But he let the man sit in the chair and hold the pole. He reeled it like a madman intermittently, coughing and hacking. Later the Polak, Wyrzevski was his name, altered his will to include Fontaine. He left him a lamp, the base of which was a hand-painted, pipe-smoking sailor. It used to sit on Fontaine's bed stand, gnome-like and enigmatic with its smile, driving Galadriel's anger with its very presence.

Hidden now, the plaster sailor slept beneath a sweater and old lo mein boxes.

Yet among the complexities of captain Fontaine, his greatest paradox, perhaps greater than his ability to be completely mad yet run his business with admirable efficiency, was the legendary status he had reached as a navigator despite the most profound shortcoming imaginable for a man of the sea.

Summer people, in the hot months that smelt more like dogwood and hycinthias than salt and wind, crammed the docks with sun fish and schooners and speedboats and jet-skis and other idle contraptions of the rich. Anyone determined to reach open ocean had to navigate the Swatch, a narrow inlet that was not quite a bay. Some spots were only a foot or so deep during low tide and the passage could get choppy and dark at a moment's notice, tips of submerged rocks peering out like periscopes of enemy submarines.

No one could navigate the Swatch like Fontaine. He bobbed and weaved around the straight better than any other sailor on the Cape. It was not uncommon to find a train of younger captains hauling out behind the *Glory Hound*, mirroring his path. Sometimes they'd delay their trips if Fontaine ran late or strand a late patron on the docks clutching a six pack because the day was particularly choppy and they didn't have enough confidence to shoot through the Swatch without Fontaine's lead. Word of the phenomenon stretched to all over ports from Falmouth to Provincetown and as far east as New Bedford.

Unknown to Fontaine, this innate sense of direction was his only inheritance, besides the boat, from his water-logged father. In his infancy Fontaine had been quite attached to the buoyant, adventuresome man who'd sired him. When he was taken on deck by his mother that final time, along with their family and many of the other captains, he'd stared silently out with the same panoramic stare, all the way to the spot where his father had been dragged off his own boat in the clutches of a spring squall. After that the route was forever burned into his memory. When he doodled he'd draw it in all its variation according to wind and moon and stars without any knowledge of what he was really doing, scrawling maps worth thousands of dollars across yesterday's funny pages, loops and hooks and zigzags.

But the great shortcoming was that Fontaine never caught any fish.

He used to. Shortly after high school when he'd put the boat in the water for the first time in sixteen years he reeled in stripers and albacore and makos and every other slippery beast in the sea. They met their end and bled on the point of his gaff. Then he'd married Galadriel and the children followed. The ocean lost its purpose as a companion for him and he took to hooking rich people instead. Much to the other Captain's annoyance and shame, this worked beyond his wildest dreams. Fontaine believed himself the happiest man on earth.

But it had been Galadriel who'd wrung the purpose out of Fontaine. Now he was left to continue his profession hollowly, like a priest who'd lost his faith administering communion.

Alone at the bar in Hooters, surrounded by wood paneling and satellite sports channels, Captain Fontaine smirked into his beer.

"Captain?" Candy said.

Like all the girls she wore a tight, garish outfit of white and orange, face painted into a mask of desire. Their chatter and bright colors reminded Fontaine of parrots. All of them called him Captain, fondly, as did everyone, a phenomenon which created a decidedly unfounded (especially in his delicate condition) air of authority about him, leading people to consult him on all types of matters, from marriage counseling to pet care, in which he had no business giving advice on.

Fontaine was hardly aware of their reverence anyway. In his mind he merely chose to drink his beer and chat amiably with anyone who cared to, locals or game, and slowly stew in the juices of the madness that kept him sleeping in that queen-size junkyard that smelled, if he tried hard enough, like the ghost of Galadriel's body, undercut with tinges of sadness, solitude, sweat, and soy sauce.

"Captain?" Candy repeated. "That man sent this over here."

She slid him a Heineken. Fontaine smiled, straight rows of white teeth glistening. Candy returned her own smile, delicate and falsely bashful and sashayed away into the kitchen.

Fontaine raised his head. At the end of the dark, varnished bar sat a smartly dressed man of about forty-five, with a leisurely tan as dark as his own but owning none of the same rugged quality. He was handsome in a dangerous way and several of the waitresses fawned over him, brewing private dreams of being whisked away to live on movie sets or in southern mansions. The most peculiar thing was his fingers. They glittered with rings of all types: silver, gold, platinum, some bearing dark stones, others simple bands. They clinked on his bottle when he drank, and when he did he drank deep, pulling on his beer until it was half gone, feigning a sheepish grin as if in wonder at his voracious thirst.

"He's rich," Candy mouthed conspiratorially. She was new and had yet to realize that everyone on the Cape was either rich or depressed that they weren't. Nothing about this man exuded depression.

Fontaine sent a fresh beer ahead of him toward that end of the bar, then trailed it slowly, pausing to chat with other regulars, all men, all slightly more pathetic than him in some way, if not only for the way they fondled each waitress with their eyes, breaching every curve, while he kept staring in his strange way past them, at everything all at once. That was part of the reason why the girls liked him so much and helped him field his quarry.

"El Capitan!" said the man, raising his glass, sloshing beer out of it. "You didn't need to send this."

Fontaine shrugged, sat next to the man. "Hear you want to catch some fish," Fontaine added, needing none of the silly banter he usually engaged in about the Red Sox or the stock market, which he only pretended to understand. He was good with people in a direct way, impersonal and efficient without being cold.

"Sharks," the man said blankly, expecting some response from Fontaine, something of incredulity or impressiveness.

Fontaine had seen a million and five sharks in his lifetime. "Heard you get mostly blues out here," he added.

"Sure, we'd probably get blues," Fontaine said, avoiding, as always, a direct lie. "We could get makos too and some threshers, but blues the most. Can't tell, you never know what's down there."

The man smiled and spread his hands at Fontaine, rings glittering. Some fingers were three or four rings deep. "Thing is, I have a damn boat! I need a *Captain*! I have a yacht and some pansy ass, fruit wearing, short-shorts, putts it up and down the canal for me. Big *shit*!"

And he ordered shots of tequila, which they drank together. Fontaine detested tequila, but trolling for dollars forced him to drink all manner of alcohol that he detested and they blended into one fiery liquid that he sucked down without joy or relish, but with the resolve of workmanship. After an hour, he'd worked himself into a fervent drunkenness, along with the man, who had bought all the tequila and Coronas in the bar, as well as, supposedly, the southeasterly quarter of Cuttyhunk.

"Don't worry. I'm leaving it just the way it is. It's just part of the collection," the man said. He wiggled the rings in Fontaine's face. "Bet you're wondering what these are all about," he said.

Before Fontaine had briefly wondered, but now he only watched the room spin and buzz. The man chuckled to himself and made no attempt to explain the comment.

Fontaine raised his eyebrows.

"I wonder too sometimes," the man said cryptically. "Must be nice, you know, simple, on the ocean, you against the fish."

"Lishen," Fontaine slurred, then recovered himself. "Once, this bachelor party books a trip. Ten men, none of them fishing, just getting blitzed and puking over the side of the boat and sleeping on the deck. That night, the dads and uncles and cousins all pass out. I cut through the cabin to get to the head. Two shapes are moving around under the blankets like tomcats in a potato sack. I say 'holy shit' just out of basic nature. Then the groom-to-be and the best man poke their heads out.

"Please mister, don't tell anyone" he begs. I close the door of the head behind me."

"You tell the wife?"

Fontaine paused dramatically out of instinct, unaware of what a good storyteller he was.

"She met them at the docks. Asked what they caught. I told her only thing we managed to get were a couple of rainbow trout."

The man guffawed, holding his belly.

"Ain't what you think out there," Fontaine said honestly.

"You take cash?" the man asked.

Fontaine thought about what he'd like to be paid in. He'd like to be paid in moments with his wife. He wished this man could take out his wallet and withdraw kisses and movies on the couch together like dollar bills from its folds.

"Say there," a man sidled up to the two of them. A handlebar moustache hung under his nose. He wore a denim jacket and was roughly the size and shape of a keg of beer.

"Tolliver," Fontaine acknowledged. Tolliver was, in fact, the anti-Fontaine. His patrons caught loads of fish, hauled them in by the bucketful. He ate smoked striper for breakfast, codfish cakes for lunch and mako steaks for dinner. But Tolliver failed to attract the money which Fontaine so easily angled. He couldn't understand this dynamic and pored over it nightly as he watched Fontaine at the bar, sucking in the clients like a baleen whale. Tolliver would never figure that out while he pitched a guarantee of slimy, bloody fish to his clients, Fontaine's mere demeanor pitched the carefree, adventurous lifestyle each man yearned for secretly since boyhood.

"So, you gonna take this fellow here shark fishing but you ain't going to tell him 'bout the tourney?" Tolliver asked, leering.

In actuality, Fontaine himself had forgotten about the tournament long ago. Twenty years it had been going on. In the early days, before Galadriel, he fished it and put up respectable poundage. Once he placed second.

"Tournament?" the rich guy asked.

"Oak Bluffs *Monster* Shark Tourney," Tolliver said slowly, emphasizing the word monster. "On ESPN and everything, 'bout two-hundred-fifty boats." The squat man narrowed his eyes. Fontaine, as expected, merely sipped his beer and shrugged, but the billionaire was hooked.

"Three day trip," Fontaine said blithely, swirling the dregs of his beer, "Little more expensive."

Tolliver had already debated to himself whether to seduce the rich guy to fish on his own boat or to let Fontaine suffer such crushing embarrassment that it would surely ruin his business on the Cape. Banking that Fontaine would trap himself, he staved off his greed and settled for the latter. Tolliver watched with relish as Fontaine goaded the man into booking the trip with careless affectations, nods of the heads, shrugs, and throwaway mentions of fish the size of French armoires. He'd seen this dance before, from his regular booth in the corner behind a pile of chicken bones and jealousy.

"Prize is a 31' Fountain with twin 225 horsepower Mercury outboards plus the trailer," Tolliver chimed, salivating, "Gear like that'll run a man a hundred and a half, likely."

"My membership might've run out," Fontaine said into his glass. Competitors needed to belong to the Boston Big Game Fishing Club, the group that organized the tournament. "Actually, it did."

Tolliver thought fast. "Well, if the boy here wants a shark in July he ought to fish the tourney. Shame not to. Tell you what, I'll let you use mine."

Fontaine raised his eyebrows, seemingly about to protest, but suddenly winked at the rich man. "Well, I guess that's all up to the big guy."

"You bet your ass it is," the man replied grinning. He ordered another round of Buds, since they'd drunk all the Heinekens and Coronas. Asia, the black girl, ran up the street to buy more Cuervo at the man's behest, a hundred dollar bill in her fist. Fontaine sighed, letting the booze carry his mind away to a place that was not the immediate present, filling up his consciousness with the fog that carried him through each day.

At some time during the night he left the bar in a stupor, strolling down the empty streets, gazing at the replica street lamps and wheelbarrows on the lawns and thinking of nothing at all, for nothing seemed different than any other trip he had booked. The captain had not owned his own car in over a decade, and so walked everywhere, savoring the sound of his feet against the ground, imagining the hot center of the earth miles below his feet. The image of Galadriel chugging away in the minivan crossed his mind and for the briefest moment his eyes watered before the madness evaporated his tears.

Somehow, before he knew it, he was in his garbage heap of a bed. Days passed without distinction as he rose and fell with the sun, eating burgers and Buffalo wings. He polished and primed the boat, ground chum, froze mackerel, lounged in the air-conditioned cockpit of his boat while men with sweaters tied around their shoulders drank gin and tonics and held the fishing equipment gingerly, like a gun with the safety off. The wet spring began to dry out, the grass turned brown, and suddenly fireworks were going off over Buzzard's Bay. Galadriel had not returned, and Fontaine no longer answered his mother's phone calls about the children. When the man called to confirm the trip, speaking in brisk phrases like punches, Fontaine vaguely recalled the encounter, as his madness was in such an advanced state. Of course, it was posted in his date book in scratchy, rear-leaning scrawl. There was no denying the trip was a reality. On the appointed day he readied his boat, unprepared for anything spectacular.

All mornings are gray. Eventually they may ascend into a pink, slivery, blossoming skylight, ever shading into the electric-blue of true daylight, but they are all born equal. On July seventeenth the man arrived in a gigantic SUV called a Minotaur that Fontaine had never even heard of. The rich man stumbled into the gray of three-thirty a.m. wearing wrinkled shorts and a tattered baseball cap, a small bag slung over his arm and a large cooler in his fist.

"Which one's the boat?" the man squinted at the docks, listening to the other boats knock against them. Fontaine pointed out the *Glory Hound*.

For seasoned fishermen, shark fishing is a kind of cakewalk. The plan was to coast along the northeast end of Martha's Vineyard, dripping chum in crooked, oily streaks for miles, dragging chunks of mackerel and garrulous flocks of gulls behind them. Fontaine explained it all before to the man over the phone, after he'd set up their entrance fee and mooring and check-in, so that they'd get to begin fishing directly instead of motoring all the way in to Oak Bluffs and back out again before dawn. They loaded clothes, beer, and sandwich meat onto the boat. Fontaine brought some tequila even though he liked to keep hard liquor out of the picture. Too unpredictable, but in some cases called for.

"Which ones can we eat? The man asked, easing into the fighting chair.

"Any but the blues, really," Fontaine said. "In a bind, though, I guess you'd eat any of them."

"Make's Mother Nature happy to eat what you kill," the man said, hands behind his head, eyes invisible beneath his sunglasses. "Some kind of Indian mumbo-jumbo-balance bullshit, right?"

Fontaine's newest customer was unaware that running a vessel like the *Glory Hound* usually required two people. Steering against the winds and tides and wills of the elements, cutting chum, hacking chunk bait, pulling and letting lines, all took valuable attention. Fontaine always managed everything himself. When his catch dropped off he'd fired Arnold, his old Swedish deck hand. He realized that this person was still just *the rich guy* in his head. He'd paid with a sharp-looking stack of hundreds that Fontaine quietly locked away in a place no one else on planet earth knew about.

"I just realized I don't know your name."

"Caldwell," Caldwell said, jerking a thumb at his chest, not knowing Fontaine's name himself but too proud to ask. "Now start that fucking engine," he said in a very friendly way. The engines rumbled, the briny water gurgled beneath them, and they churned their way toward the horizon, well on its way to not being gray anymore.

Caldwell spent the first six hours sleeping violently in the cabin, making thumps and thwacks and bumps and grunts against the door, sounding much like a blue or a thresher galumphing beneath the hull. Fontaine didn't care. He was alone, passing the time as he always did, looking forward to the night, when he could gaze at the coast of the Vineyard, invisible to the untrained eye, like the buried spine of some ancient dinosaur. The lights would be like stars sunken into the ocean, the eyes of mermaids gazing out Atlantis's basement window.

The day was sprinkled with wet, salty showers.

Choppy waves lapped over the gunwales. *So much like a woman*, thought Fontaine, staring at his hands, shell-like with calluses from the lines. Such a guise, to behave so human, and he wondered the same of his wife and children and of their unimaginable alien depths, his madness burning deep in the nastiest parts of his guts.

They caught no fish. He followed birds and currents and the sun but no menacing fins broke water. Once he glimpsed a right whale, black and ugly, lolling about like a slow child in the street. And he spotted the floppy, unstable fin of a sunfish, often confused with sharks, though the fish can hardly stay upright, so large and disc-like that it flops like a poorly thrown Frisbee in the waves. Fontaine went through the motions anyway, hacking, cutting, tying, rinsing spill from the chum off the deck. Any idiot can catch a shark, he thought. Drop blood and guts into the water and let them follow the scent. Wait for them to snap up one of the hooks. Drag them along with the boat until they get tired enough to stop caring if they live. Stick a gaff in their neck when they come up. It all came down to chance, really. Fontaine just had bad chances. He'd fallen into Tolliver's trap unaware. Even if he were, he wouldn't care.

At three in the afternoon Caldwell emerged from the cabin, rosy cheeked and stiff-legged, stretching, rings glittering on his fingers. He retired silently to a chair on the deck for a couple of hours, presumably sleeping beneath his mirrored glasses, but when he spoke it was sudden.

"What've we got?"

"Nothing," Fontaine responded, hacking bait methodically. He shrugged. "They eat their own, you know. Sometimes they'll even take chunks out of themselves when they're in a frenzy. Don't even know the difference. They don't chew. Just tear and swallow, all gone."

"That's some shit," Caldwell clapped Fontaine on the back, rings clattering. "You got yourself a trophy room?"

"No," Fontaine answered, "I don't think that's quite natural."

"What's your favorite part then, if it ain't to show everyone else up at the sport?"

Madness is a strange, beguiling thing. It lurks, it sleeps, it stalks beneath everyday life, its ridged back humping lackadaisically out of reality's surface every so often, shocking and bizarre.

Fontaine grasped Caldwell's hand and pinned it tightly to the board with a grip hardened by years of holding whizzing steel lines against the blood and bone of his palm. He raised the knife high above his head. It whistled on the way down.

Clink!

A twisted, broken ring clinked to the deck. Caldwell stood silent, gazing at his naked finger in disbelief.

"Bone knife," Fontaine remarked placidly. He kept hacking at frozen scup. "I'm real precise with it," he said. Caldwell watched, still stunned, as he cut the fish into exact, even chunks, perfect ovals until they became flaky messes under the water. For Fontaine, in his madness, this was a completely appropriate response to Caldwell's question.

"That was my wedding ring," he said calmly, regaining his wits but leery.

"Looks to me you got ones to spare," Fontaine replied jovially.

"My trophy room," Caldwell said calmly, flashing them again in the sun. Fontaine stopped hacking to get beers. They rested together on a bench and opened canned Coronas, the sky now the magical color of a lonely stripper.

"These rings," he said, wiggling his fingers. "All married women, one sort or another. I know what you're thinking," he said quickly, "I'm some con man taking advantage of rich old ladies, bringing them down to Panama or Brussels and then plucking their withered little prune-hearts out with an ice pick." Caldwell slurped his beer in his usual voracious chug.

"No sir, I don't discriminate young from old, rich from poor, white from black," Caldwell crushed his beer can and dragged another one out from beneath the melting ice in the cooler. "Say something nice to them the first time you see them, say, on the street, or in a restaurant. Make a few clandestine phone calls, arrange a trip somewhere exciting, fuck their brains out, say goodbye. No false promises from me." He was already half done with his second beer.

"The rings?" Fontaine asked, eyes blanketing the horizon.

"Husbands," Caldwell said coldly. "Sad bastards, those guys. Bottom feeders, senators, garbage-men. Suckers, all of 'em. Take your pick."

Fontaine's shirt rippled in the breeze.

"They *give* them to me. That's my price. Tell her she'll be the next ring on this finger, she's going to take it right off hubby in the middle of the night just because I asked her to, sneak it over to me. They do it. You know why they do it?"

Fontaine shook his head no.

"Want to prove to themselves they won't. Like a challenge. Show them how many others couldn't keep away. I tell them right off."

"Bait," Fontaine uttered.

"Yeah you get it," Caldwell said. "Long time ago something happened to me with a woman, almost ruined me. I'm doing these fellows a favor "That's why I make them take the rings, see? Kills the promise. I'm setting them free."

He held up the chunk of metal. "Nicked up a nice one here. Worth seeing you chop like that, though."

I found a ring once," Fontaine said blandly. "Down in a tuna's guts. It was a great old ring, huge, green with rot from the acid in its belly. Could have been straight off Poseidon's finger, all I knew about it."

"You got it now?"

"Threw it back in the ocean," Fontaine half lied. He'd showed it to Galadriel on their final anniversary. The ring was too big to replace her wedding band, like he wanted. He wrapped it in a scallop shell with a bow of seaweed and told her that he would wear it. She threw it back in the ocean, said that was where it belonged. Fontaine marked the spot with unrivaled precision and paid some teenager with a scuba tank fifty bucks to retrieve it. The ring lay swaddled in an old bandana at the bottom of his pocket.

It was Caldwell's turn now to remain silent and he complied, maintaining that vacant reverence some people with money bestow on those with less. Generous in their importance, they pass it like a joint and let its aura fill the room.

"Wouldn't believe what they find in a shark's guts," Fontaine ventured, spurred by Caldwell's graciousness. "All types of jewelry. Chains and torpedoes and erector sets, suits of armor. And that's just the stuff that sticks around."

"Eating machines," Caldwell said.

"Eat anything on earth."

A gull cawed here or there. Caldwell could not find it on the open water, but Fontaine knew it was due east.

"Let me take the wheel a while," Caldwell said, thumping Fontaine on the shoulder, without the slightest hint the Captain was fantasizing about hacking him to pieces with the bone knife.

"C'mon, you damned tiger."

He grabbed some lines and hooks and set to work.

"Better watch it, I'm a wild one," Fontaine joked.

Caldwell chuckled and pounded the side of the boat again, pulling a beer from nowhere. He climbed into the cockpit and goosed the throttle, scaring away whatever fish might be around.

"Run us south for a bit. We'll get close to Nantucket Sound for tomorrow.

We can sleep right out here." To his surprise Caldwell obeyed wordlessly, as though he were nothing more than a young mate. Now and then he barked out navigational questions in a tone so serious it was almost caricature. But Fontaine could tell his rapt attention was genuine.

The Captain laid back in the fighting chair setting a line with his agile fingers. He reached out for a chunk of mackerel and saw, clearly, his brown fingers stretched against the clear blue of the ocean, their hardy grace broken with a white line where he used to wear the ring. Galadriel and the children floated to the top of his mind like a poisonous jellyfish he wanted to hold in his arms. He thought of Caldwell's shining fingers clutched tight against the wheel. The bone knife lay on the deck next to him.

In that moment Captain Fontaine could have easily sunk the blade into the thick meat between Caldwell's neck and shoulder blade. He did not. Captain Fontaine unfolded the old bandana, which smelled of engine grease, and set the old, huge, green ring at the end of the line instead of the mackerel. Then he pitched it into the foamy wake.

"Bait," he said aloud, thinking of Caldwell's rings. He kicked the bone knife away.

Caldwell insisted on sleeping in the open air of the deck until he was slimed over with the night mist of the ocean. He retreated grouchily to the cabin. He'd wanted to be close to the lines in case of a hit. Fontaine slept in the cockpit, rocked to sleep by the familiar listing of the boat from starboard to port, fingers draped loosely across the wheel. He was awakened by an unfamiliar sound, soft but sharp, like the whisper of an old friend thought long dead.

Under the gentle lapping of the waves, Fontaine woke to the sound of a line hissing.

The captain raced to the chair, grabbing the rod with a sweeping motion and buckling himself in all at once. Overexcited, he hit the fish immediately and the line went slack. He sat for a heart wrenching moment of doubt, but the line went out again and he let it go, waiting, hitting infrequently and with caution, reeling in greatly when he could. He screamed for Caldwell to get up and start the boat so they could tire the bastard out, but Caldwell didn't answer. There was only Fontaine and the first fish he'd been hooked to in over a decade.

For what felt like hours he struggled with the fish. Each time he was sure it was nearly dawn he'd look up at the stars overhead, marveling, but quickly forget as the line pulled taut and he tugged mightily against it. He felt the slack lengthening and pulling out in spite of the reel. Fontaine gritted his teeth and lunged backward, heaving the handle of the rod upward like an executioner readying a blow with his axe, breaking all the rules he'd ever been taught. The fish thumped against the stern.

He rose, clutching the gaff with his elbow. Below, the fish thrashed on the surface, unrecognizable.

"Caldwell!" he shrieked. No answer.

Fontaine locked the reel. He held the rod over his shoulder and sprinted for the cockpit, dragging the fish up the stern and over the stern with a final crash.

Eyes closed, hot and cool with sweat, Fontaine drank the moment like a glass of expensive wine. Like he was the Mongol horde and it were the blood of his enemies. He was too vindicated to question the stark silence in place of the thrashing and gasping the fish should be doing.

Fontaine turned.

A naked woman lay rumpled at the stern of the boat. At first he thought her dead, but then he saw her head upturned, a slight, narrow face curtained with waves of reddish brown hair cascading around her shoulders. Her skin seemed tanned and pale all at once, as though its color were only a sheen that changed with the quality of the moonlight.

She beckoned with a finger at Fontaine. He saw her hand glitter with rings, hundreds of them, as though she wore silver gloves. His eyes fell to her left hand, splayed on the deck. His ring was around her finger, still rigged up to the line he'd cast.

When he reached her, Fontaine knelt to the ground. He felt a slow pressure on his groin. The woman straddled him and he let it go without argument. It would have felt unnatural if she had not straddled him.

"Men," she said with what sounded to Fontaine like scornful worship, unbuckling his belt. She moved back and forth and he watched Galadriel's face rise out of her, leer down at him, kiss him softly. He tried to talk, but she made no sign of hearing him over her own screams and groans and wails, superficial and piercing, undulating like the cries of whales and dolphins. Her smooth skin slid over him, her face shimmered the way the sun looked from a fathom below the ocean's surface.

"The rings," he said drowsily, clasping his hands around the small of her back.

She whispered things in his ear he couldn't understand that calmed him anyway.

Her voice cooed soft and melodic, but on the verge of the sound a scream would make trapped in a bubble underwater. She slipped her tongue into his mouth and he could still hear her cries inside his head. Suddenly all he could think of were sea slugs. He tried to pull away, but she felt like a heavy sack of water on top of him. Fontaine tore his face from hers and thrust out from underneath her.

She was dripping, gleaming naked, crawling forward on all fours. Only now, her hair was mounds of kelp, her breasts shells of abalone, her eyes the reflections of the moon on the ocean. Her form shimmered, dark sand from the bottom of the world sifting from her makeshift limbs. The rings he'd seen on her hands were green and prehistoric with algae. A suckered tentacle slipped in and out from between her pulsing lips.

He lifted the bone knife from where it lay. His arm dropped. Blood spurted across his cheek, onto his forearms, growing darker, nearly black, and thicker, not running down in rivulets but clutching to him. Scales sparkled in the air like fairy dust, flying everywhere, along with flecks of bone or shells, he didn't know which. Sand gritted between his teeth and he wrapped his hands around the thing's neck as it cried out in both agony and ecstasy. The face became Galadriel's and he didn't care at all, he hacked and hacked and hacked as he felt dawn warming his back. He tore the things eyes out, and along with it his own madness, ripping it away and tossing it to float out into the sky toward the sun, which had just started to shine the orange of burnt clay.

When it was all over the deck was strewn with ooze and ragged limbs. Something glimmered. Fontaine picked up the hand, still attached to the line, and twisted it in the moonlight. He thought he saw a starfish but couldn't be sure.

Captain Fontaine tossed whatever it was back into the ocean. Only then did he finally run for the tequila.

He woke alone, covered in blackish blood and hung over in his chair, his pants unbuckled and his hat on the floor. Before his passenger woke he put down the ladder and bathed warily in the salt water. Then he hosed off the deck.

Caldwell had a serious ill humor when he finally rose. "You know how I make all my money?" he asked quietly, the sun barely up over the water, hanging as if it were about to drop back in.

"I'm a seafood distributor. I buy fish that suckers catch and I sell them to other suckers in restaurants and supermarkets, and somehow, somewhere along the line, I get all the money, I get all the fringe benefits."

Caldwell continued to relate the specific history of his money all through the morning, the thousands of things he'd bought with it, and, subtly, how it made him superior to Fontaine in every way imaginable.

"It's not like I'm better than people who don't have money," he said plaintively, palms upturned, "I'm just different. I can't help that. It's the world." Caldwell fingered the space on his finger where the ring Fontaine had chopped off once had been.

"Last night . . ." Caldwell began.

"What?"

"Nothing," he said. "It isn't that important."

One by one Fontaine checked the lines, scooping the fetid chum into the water. He came to the last one and skipped it deliberately, not wanting to know what was on the other end.

Caldwell had heard Fontaine on the deck last night, chopping and screaming like a lunatic. In the morning he woke to the smell of rotten fish and found the deck covered in pools of blood and fish meat, all stewing in the sun. The captain was hung over in the cockpit, soaked in it as well. Caldwell shuddered, thought of Fontaine's handiness with the bone knife.

Compared to the last few days, the calm was disturbing. The sea and the sky were nearly one, the horizon blurring the ocean and the atmosphere into one gaping blue hole in the fabric of the universe. The boat seemed to float in a void, save the light ripple of the wake.

Fontaine grew uneasy and impatient with the calm. He gunned the engine. As the boat accelerated he strode back to the chum bucket, lifted it, and emptied a steady stream of meat and bone and gristle and oil into the ocean behind them. Caldwell watched, entranced and frightened for one of the few times in his life. Though he'd bathed, Fontaine was still covered in scales and glittered in the sun as he climbed the tower and perched there, content.

The boat beat away at the flat ocean, running toward the sun, then beneath it, then toward it again in the evening as the deadline approached and they headed back to port, shark-less after all. Other ships were now visible, so many white flecks in the distance that they seemed like constellations and asteroids amid the deep blue.

"Some idiot caught one over there," Fontaine said. They were the first words spoken between the men since morning. "That's why they—"

Suddenly the bow heaved out of the water and the stern dipped. One of the lines hissed, the reel spinning so fast the motion barely registered. Fontaine did not need to look to know which line it was. Caldwell forgot how scared he'd become of Fontaine and cracked a beer and whooped.

"You going to take care of that?" he screamed down to Caldwell from the tower, his cap blowing off behind him into the waves, which whispered over the motor in a language that could be spoken but never understood.

In Oak Bluffs, onlookers lined the docks for the weigh-in. They wore fins on their heads or shark teeth around their neck. Small children bobbed on their fathers' shoulders, craning to see the boats march in. The water was a vivid greenish-blue, the shadows long against the pink and yellow gingerbread cottages.

For each shark that was raised the crowd sighed deeply with disbelief. A man would bark out the weight and everyone would cheer and then the process repeated itself. This went on for a long while, until the line of boats had dwindled to a small queue. Some of the older men watched the line of ships and thought of the Swatch, and how, despite being old men, they too had tacked and jigged behind Fontaine around the dangerous rocks and sandbars. And they slowly remembered that he was fishing the tourney, Tolliver had told them, with some obscenely rich person. The old men scratched their heads and wondered where Fontaine was, time was nearly up and he hadn't shown with his nothing yet.

When the *Glory Hound* finally appeared, far away on the lip of the horizon, there was something distinctly different about it, something wrong with the way it moved. As it neared, the crowd saw that it rocked to and fro, back and forth, sometimes nearly halting altogether, staggering along like a dog on a leash dragging its owner behind. All the boats had been weighed and many people had left, but the few who remained hushed. Some of them were the old men who remembered Fontaine, binoculars raised to their newspaper-colored eyes. Tolliver, too, was there, weaving in and out of the spotty crowd, exchanging jokes with men at Fontaine's expense, fingering the wax on his moustache with his thumb and forefinger like a man about to tie a woman to the railroad tracks. His loose cotton boat pants were almost frayed at the thighs from his nervous skittering.

"Probably rammed his boat up on a sandbar," he joked, elbowing someone near him.

"Fontaine ain't never rammed anything with that boat in his life," the other man replied.

"Guess we'll see," Tolliver said hungrily.

The *Glory Hound* rocked with each pull of the great fish, sprays of water shooting like geysers behind her. Fontaine blared the horn and Caldwell made deep, guttural sounds from the bottom of his chest, still strapped to the fighting chair. They'd dragged it in alive, trying to make the time, grinding gears against the cords of muscle writhing beneath the water, angry whirlpools churning in their wake.

Fontaine's madness was far gone, his mind scoured clean by the salt on the wind. Head held high, he gunned the engine and dragged the shark directly into shore instead of docking, grounding his boat, the shark thrashing about in the shallow water.

They screamed at him from shore and the other ships, calling him other names. Some children, holding balloons, slipped from their mothers' hands and sprinted to the water's edge, parents running after them and wailing. Heedlessly, Fontaine pitched over the gunwale into the shallow water, landing flatly on his heels in the sand. He waded toward the shore, then dared a glance back at the shark's roiling jaws lunging out of the water, snapping at the air, swimming in circles.

Fontaine wavered.

Millions and millions of years ago, something slimy and pallid crawled up out of the sea, something that took short, nervous breaths of air and crawled with quick, heavy steps, something that left the dependability and bounty of the ocean behind for the hot, dry earth before it. There is no greater mystery than what may have happened if that creature had balked, wavering on its jelly-like legs, and turned and submerged itself back into the safe cradle of the ocean.

He saw his boat rising like a pillar. He saw the shark, Caldwell, the crowds. All the things that had been and could be for him, here, on this ocean. Then he lifted his foot and slogged the final fifty yards to shore, tearing away his shoes and tossing them aside, picking up speed, finally running barefoot onto the beach and up to the road.

Some people followed him crying out questions, but he jostled and elbowed away. Once he made the common he was clear, hurtling through the gazebo, still barefoot, wet prints across the walkway behind him. Long after they evaporated, years even, people would point and say "That's the way Fontaine went."

A riotous uproar shook the docks. The crowd had rushed down to the beach, standing at the edge of the surf. A few men and children ventured up to their knees.

"Watch it! Don't know if I can hold him!" Caldwell called, giving the shark a little slack. Its tail clapped against the side of the boat as it sped toward the shore and people ran screaming out of the water.

Those who saw it swore the foundations of wharf shook, the wooden posts wobbling, masts of the docked boats reeling. The harbormaster called the Coast Guard, who puttered in aboard a great orange chopper and circled uselessly. Channel 6 News showed up in a van from the ferry, and all the local papers were crowded around with telephoto lenses, scribbling words in little notepads.

"That's a Great White, that's fucking Jaws," the man next to Tolliver said.

"That's just an aggressive, oversized bottle-nose," Tolliver replied with scorn. The other man laughed hard. "Didn't you lend him your slip?"

The grounded ship lurched as the tethered shark zigzagged, its belly scraping the sand. Caldwell secured the rod to the fighting chair, locked the reel, and stood, hands cupped to his ears. Some official-looking people were yelling something to him but he couldn't hear. They weren't official-looking enough to be police officers. He sat up and waved.

"Too late!" the man screamed. He wore a sleek blue suit and dark wraparound glasses. "You're too late! Weigh-in ended six minutes ago!"

A Maine lobsterman had taken the prize with a pair of four-hundred pound makos.

"Like I give a damn!" Caldwell said brazenly, chest puffed out. Not to be outdone by Fontaine, he too hurdled the gunwale and braved the water so close to the shark. "Stuff that fucker. He's going over my mantel," he said when he got to shore.

"You must have some mantel," the chief of police said to him. Practically the entire island had showed up by then.

"You have no idea."

A few miles down the road, in Vineyard Haven, a ferry was pulling away from the dock, all but empty. News traveled fast on such a small island and all the tourists and day-trippers had flocked to Oak Bluffs to see the shark. One man stood toward the stern of the ferry, watching the island recede. He had a ragged tan and silver eyes and saw the whole island at once disappearing from view.

In the days that followed no one knew what to do with the giant fish. It labored in the harbor for days, thrashing, scaring children and gulls, until it grew silent and still, its twitching tail the only sign of life. There was a great protest from PETA, crying that the shark could not be killed and some activists barely escaped with all their parts intact when they tried to free it by night. Eventually it seemed the shark had spent all the life it had on the end of that line, and the point became moot. The authorities turned the situation over to Caldwell.

"How'd you do it?" the guys from ESPN and Channel 6 asked, the local papers clutching to their backs like lamprey, their microphones thrust out like proboscis.

"That's Fontaine's fish," he said honestly. "I just did some of the legwork." He told them everything about Fontaine's episode from the bloody deck to dumping the chum and their wild rush for shore.

A young blonde from the Globe sidled up next to him, looking for nuggets for a human interest piece.

"Ian, are you a married man?" she clamored over the other reporters, a forest of microphones thrust in his face.

Caldwell smiled and held up his hand, showing them the rings, and shrugged. They jabbered more questions at him but he remained silent.

But when Caldwell's day to collect the shark arrived it was nowhere to be found. The line was coiled on the ocean floor. The hook was clean, as if it had never been embedded in the cage of knifelike teeth.

Experts from the Marine Biology Institute in Wood's Hole discovered it was, in actuality, a tiger shark, likely the biggest living known specimen. Six rows of teeth in a mouth like a vortex that consumed seals, squid, and even turtles. They said that Tiger shark's hunted by night and could navigate murky waters. They even said male tiger sharks hold the females with their teeth when mating, and, interestingly, were known as the sacred *Auma Kua,* or ancestor spirits, of Hawaiians.

They could not, however, tell anyone how the damn hook got out of the shark after holding for a good five days until the shark was all but dead.

The island emptied of its shark enthusiasts. Gradually, like always, other things became important, like the Jazz Festival or a party on the Kennedy Compound or Bill Clinton playing golf.

Fontaine was never seen on Cape Cod or the islands again. His small boat was dragged out of the harbor with a winch and left to rot on the shore, since no one would pay to remove it. Not even Caldwell, who told them they should put a plaque on it and make it a monument. The boat got so bleached and barren white that people came to call it the *Ghost,* the original name long faded from the hull and forgotten. It remained long after people forgot to call it anything. During a serious hurricane season the waves smashed it into driftwood and shattered plastic that looked like broken teeth in the sand.

But Fontaine's legend never died. When ships left the Swatch and followed some other more experienced sailor they still called it Fontaining. His spectacular exit impacted the darker superstitions that sailors are prone to carry and became canonical. On the decks of some ships, more than most would like to admit, when a great fish was hooked unexpectedly, out of nowhere, almost luckily, that it was in actuality the madness Captain Fontaine had shed that caught the line, and it must be cut immediately and the entire chum bucket be dumped behind the boat. A commercial schooner from New Bedford lost a great load of cod when they pulled up some unimaginable creature in their nets and a squat man swore in Portuguese *Esta Fontaine! Mal, mal!* They unhinged it and let it drop down toward the unimaginable depths, where everything foul and membranous lurked, mouths wide and full of teeth.

The night he'd wrecked his boat, Fontaine had snuck onto the ferry with little trouble. In Hyannis he walked home to Apple Blossom Road and extracted every item from his home. He piled them high beneath the swing-set, red and rusty, and doused it with gasoline. By the time he arrived at Hooters the underbelly of the sky was lit with his old life. He smiled to himself and entered. The bar was close to empty, some elderly folks picking at their food in the booths.

"Come with me," he said to Candy with a wild look in his eye that she had never seen. Candy walked outside with him.

"Let's get out of here," he said.

"What do you mean?" she asked nervously. She thought he was being inappropriate. She worked at Hooter's, but she wasn't a whore. But she knew Fontaine, so she heard him out.

Fontaine didn't have any answer, but he took her hand anyway.

"You got a car?" he asked. He waited for her to nod.

He didn't show her the wad of cash in his wallet, Caldwell's ludicrous down payment for the trip. He wanted her to come of her own accord. He didn't want to use any bait. "I just want someone to go somewhere with me," he explained.

Candy, in her sweet, earnest innocence, grasped the dream of every Hooter's girl in Fontaine's callused palm, and they were gone, her buxom orange shorts bouncing in the mounting darkness. Later, in Ohio, Fontaine watched the land roll away behind him. Candy spoke as she drove, but her words did not matter. He listened to the news about himself on the radio. Everything was about the shark.

"We have to go back," he said. Candy looked at him, upset.

"Not for long," he said.

It was his debt to repay. Fontaine showed up at the night's zenith, at its blackest, when the town was asleep. He'd had a couple of drinks in a bar on the corner before heading down to the beach, where he slipped off all of his clothes and slid into the water.

Next to the boat the shark swirled its tail, resting. He walked up to it confidently, stroked its rough skin, felt ripples around him from its motion.

Slowly, carefully, Fontaine's hand crept toward its mouth. From his waistband he pulled the bone knife, flat and dull in the darkness, with the other hand. Then found the mouth, gently opened it and found the hook. In the end he didn't need the knife, the hook slid gently out of its jaws, as if for days it had not been hooked, but clenching tightly on the line. The hook was bare, his ring gone.

Fontaine watched it go, a soft wake trailing behind.

One day years later, a rich man like Caldwell caught himself a tiger shark off of Oahu. The man, so far past the scope of this story that his name is unimportant, brought the shark to a great taxidermist, also with an unimportant name. The taxidermist took the shark hesitantly, like all the animals he stuffed. Gazelles and jackrabbits, black bears, armadillos, he'd stuffed them all. Now, during his Hawaiian retirement, he'd turned to fish. This taxidermist hated hunting and abhorred violence, but found that his profession gave him a kind of peace. He took solace in the respect he was paying to these animals that had been destroyed so cruelly and made quite a lot of money doing it. He had spectacles that sat on his nose. Many people thought he looked like Gepetto, from the old fairy tale.

He imagined the hunt as he unzipped the shark's belly and the organs slid out and onto the floor. Shark hunts, he'd come to know, were nothing more than dumping clouds of blood into the ocean and waiting for the sharks to inevitably show. Quickly, before their stink began to spread, he loaded the soft guts into a steel pail, their last stop before the pet food factory.

Something clattered, like stones knocking together. He made a note of it and moved on.

In the stomach, he found a license plate, a helium tank, and what could have been a sword. He found the remains of a smaller shark and the shell of a sea turtle. Still unsettled by the noise and the gleam he'd seen earlier, he searched the pail again, still coming up short. Wary that tiger sharks had reputations as man eaters, he looked diligently for signs of human anatomy but found none.

After two more hours he remembered the clatter and found the ring, round and green.

The taxidermist held them in his hand, tested their weight, scraped away their film to see the colorless metal underneath. As he did so he dreamed that the shark had found Atlantis and devoured a great princess there, with kelp for hair and breasts of abalone, and a voice like the ocean wind.

THE MER-MONKEY

Paul A. Freeman

In the storage room of the City Museum, Simon Murdock, the diminutive, dark-skinned curator, led his visitor through a clutter of long forgotten exhibits. They stepped over the barrel of a sixteenth century cannon and they circumvented a twenty-fifth dynasty Egyptian sarcophagus. Finally, the two men arrived at their destination—at the object of their sortie into what Murdock termed the museum's 'dingy dungeon'.

"It's a mer-monkey," said the curator, indicating a shriveled up little corpse inside a display case. "You'd be amazed at what you sometimes come across in the neglected backwater of the main museum."

The visitor was Professor Charles Renfrew, a young Oxford don often described in the press as an 'extreme anthropologist'. His expeditions to the most far-flung parts of the globe were legendary.

Renfrew squinted through the dust-smeared glass of the display cabinet. Unhappy with the view, he took a handkerchief from his jacket pocket, wiped away a circle of grime and peered in. The desiccated specimen inside certainly had the head of a monkey—a small, tree-dwelling primate by the looks of it. The teeth however, were totally unlike any monkey or ape he had ever seen. They were sharp, pointed, fearsome looking.

"The mer-monkey survives on a piscivorous diet," the curator announced, as if he had read the anthropologist's mind.

"It's a fish feeder, living in freshwater lakes—which explains the evolution of the tail."

"Ah! Yes! The tail?" said Professor Renfrew, still not entirely convinced by the exhibit. His keen eyes searched the midriff of the mummified creature for signs of stitching where the torso joined the scaly tail section. There were none, however.

The curator's face took on a predatory grin. He knew he now had the undivided interest of a world famous anthropologist, a man renowned for his discoveries of obscure animal species.

"Where exactly would I find a live specimen of a mer-monkey?" Renfrew asked, his eyes glinting avariciously in the near darkness of the dingy dungeon.

Simon Murdock scratched his chin and considered the anthropologist's question. "Have you heard of Professor Henry Armitage, the Victorian explorer and adventurer?"

"Of course I have."

"Well, on Armitage's third trip to Africa he detailed the discovery of this mer-monkey in his journal. In fact, he even mentions the creature's exact location."

The Oxford don again stared through the glass-sided display case at the mysterious mer-monkey. Finally his mind was made up. "Supposing one wished to acquire Professor Armitage's journal. The one from his third African expedition. Where would one obtain such a document?"

The curator coughed discreetly into the one hand and meaningfully held out the other, palm upwards. "I locked Armitage's journal away in the museum safe after I found it during an earlier storeroom foray."

"Isn't it a bit of a coincidence, though," said Renfrew, his incredulity difficult to dismiss. "I mean, it's strange that the mer-monkey specimen and the journal are both discovered down here in the storeroom, isn't it?"

Murdock stooped over the display cabinet and looked down ruefully at the withered, century-and-a-half old corpse lying within it. The leathery hide was drawn tight over a simian skull, and a rib poked out through the moth eaten hide. The lower part of the body was better preserved though, the scaly skin still retaining its silvery sheen.

"The reason the mer-monkey and the journal were both discovered in my little dungeon," explained the curator, "is because Professor Armitage donated both items to the City Museum on his death in 1901. They've been here in the storeroom ever since. However, as I intimated to you during our correspondence, the journal's yours—for a price."

Since receiving the curator's letter a week ago, Renfrew had more than half expected such a scenario. It wouldn't be the first time the anthropologist had paid to gain a decisive edge over his academic competitors. So he produced the wad of money he carried around with him for just such an occasion and slapped it into the other man's open palm.

"Let me get that journal for you," said the grinning curator, leading the way out of the storage room.

***

Under the guise of a backpacking tourist, Renfrew flew into Khartoum airport in northern Sudan. Early the following morning he took a southbound train.

The landscape gradually changed as the rail journey progressed, transforming from rocky desert to grassland to subtropical forest. The people changed in nature too, from dark-skinned African-Arabs in the north of the country, to sleek, black-skinned Nilotic Africans in the south.

At the railway line's southernmost terminal, Renfrew disembarked. Gone were the mosques and the five daily prayer calls of the Islamic north. Instead, the prayer call was replaced by the tolling knells of a church bell.

The relatively remote town Renfrew found himself in was still some distance from his final destination, so as the Oxford don followed in the footsteps of Henry Armitage, the Victorian explorer, he now took a rickety bus to a small village on the Congo border. The tarmac road ended and it was at this terminus that the anthropologist met Bol Karanga, the man who was to become his guide and translator.

As Renfrew got down from the bus and rubbed the numbness from his backside, a crowd of tall, black-complexioned hawkers surrounded him. One wanted to carry his backpack (for an undisclosed fee), another wanted to direct the scientist to whatever passed as a hotel in this border outpost; yet others tried foisting roasted corn cobs, wafer biscuits and warm soda drinks on the visitor.

Then the clamour around the anthropologist subsided into an uneasy silence as a squat, coffee-skinned man cut a swath through the throng. The hawkers backed away from the Westerner, muttering to one another in tones that were at the same time both fearful and angry.

"Don't pay any heed to these rip-off merchants, sir," the little man said in perfect English. "They won't be bothering you anymore. The problem is they think every white man is as rich as Rockefeller. They'll extort cash from you for even the most basic service."

Renfrew's apparent saviour held out his hand. "I'm Bol Karanga, a member of the Yinka tribe. My people live beside Lake Pio, not far from here."

The professor shook the man's outstretched hand and introduced himself. He felt doubly blessed by Bol's timely appearance. Not only had the Yinka tribesman's intervention prevented Renfrew from falling victim to the pettiest of petty criminals, but according to Armitage's journal Bol's people lived in the vicinity of the mer-monkeys' natural habitat of Lake Pio.

As Bol Karanga, with the scientist's backpack slung over his shoulder, led Renfrew to the only hotel in the out-of-the-way settlement, the professor had a few questions for his new friend.

"How come you just happened to be at the bus stop when I arrived?" he asked. "And where did you learn such good English?"

Bol explained: "In my younger days I worked as a tour guide in Khartoum. I showed embassy staff the Islamic sites of the city and the Pharaonic temples dotted around northern Sudan. Since English was their common tongue, I learned the language on the job. As for my being at the bus station, the only Westerners passing through this neck of the woods are either travelers on their way to the Congo, or anthropologists wanting to study the ethnically unique tribes around Lake Pio. I make it my responsibility to take care of their needs."

"Then it appears this time you've bagged yourself an anthropologist," laughed Renfrew, just as a one-storey, breezeblock building—advertising itself as a hotel—came into view.

***

The following day Bol Karanga prevailed upon a lorry driver to take himself and Professor Renfrew to the shores of Lake Pio. At first the man was reluctant to oblige, saying he had a return run to Khartoum. However a small fortune in foreign currency soon changed his mind.

The driver picked his way along rutted bush roads, the branches of forest trees slapping against the sides of the lorry. Eventually, on the banks of Lake Pio, with fishermen in dugouts casting their nets, Bol instructed the driver to halt.

"These Nilotic people are uncomfortable coming into our territory," the Yinka tribesman confided in his guest. "They fear us because we're so ethnically different to them."

"We all have our racial preconceptions," Renfrew sympathised, climbing down from the cab and shouldering his backpack.

Twenty minutes later the two men entered Bol's home village. Children with emaciated bodies and bulbous heads swamped Renfrew, rushing about his feet and squealing with excitement. Outside the mud-walled, thatched huts of the settlement, women pounding grain stopped in their exertions and curiously eyed their Western visitor.

Leaving his backpack at the cluster of huts belonging to Bol's family, the anthropologist strolled down to the lakeside with Bol to meet the village headman.

At the shoreline, a tiny, white-haired old man was directing fishing operations. He proved to be the headman. With Bol acting as translator, Renfrew explained the reason for his visit.

"I'm searching for the legendary mer-monkey," he said. "I have an old journal in my possession which says the mer-monkey is indigenous to Lake Pio. I'll richly reimburse you and your people if you help me locate a specimen."

Once a price had been arranged and a sum of money handed over, the Yinka headman led Professor Renfrew and Bol Karanga along the shoreline until they came to a lagoon. All the while, the dugout fishing boats kept pace with the trio.

Finally the headman halted. He pointed towards the lagoon and jabbered away to Bol in a dialect unintelligible to Renfrew.

"This is where the mer-monkeys reside," Bol translated. "You're free to wade into the water and collect a specimen."

The anthropologist took off his shoes and socks, but hesitated to enter the water.

The headman laughed and spoke to Bol.

Bol nodded. "He says you shouldn't be afraid, Mr. Renfrew. Although mer-monkeys are carnivorous, they only consume fish."

Thus reassured, dreaming of the plaudits and the fame awaiting him on his return to England with a mer-monkey specimen, the scientist waded into the lake.

Waist deep in the clear water, Renfrew shaded his eyes against the glare of the sun and searched the lagoon for any sign of a mer-monkey. A few fish swam past, but nothing remotely resembling the shrivelled up creature he had seen in the City Museum display case.

'Plop! Plop!' There suddenly came the sound of large bodies dropping into the water.

Renfrew looked up in surprise and found the grinning Yinka fishermen leaping from their dugouts into the waters of Lake Pio. Then, before the anthropologist's astonished eyes the men transformed, shrinking down in size into living versions of the mummified mer-monkey he had seen at the City Museum. Flicking their tails, they swam towards the hapless professor, their jaws chomping.

Renfrew turned, headed back in panic for the shore and saw Bol Karanga and the headman walking into the water to meet him. He thought at first they were rushing to his aid, but moments later they too changed from their human guise into sharp-toothed mer-monkeys.

The anthropologist barely had time to scream before keen little teeth started nipping off chunks of his flesh.

***

A month later, at the City Museum in England, Simon Murdock, the dark-skinned curator, received a letter from home. His brother, Bol Karanga, thanked him for sending money and food to the clan. The headman, Bol explained, praised him for being a good son.

Satisfied that he had fulfilled his filial duties, Murdock set to work on making a second forgery of Henry Armitage's journal. When the document was ready, he would write a letter to Maxwell, the famous Cambridge anthropologist, inviting him to see City Museum's mer-monkey - in reality the withered up corpse of Murdock's great grandfather - in a storeroom display cabinet.

Humans are so gullible, thought Murdock soaking newly prepared journal pages in black tea to age them.

Today he had plenty of time to work on Armatige's journal, for outside it was raining heavily. The last thing the curator wanted was to get soaked.

HEAVY WEATHER

Murphy Edwards

Tobias Kunkhe flopped his gear on the deck of the 'Stormy Weather' and hocked a lewgy into the turd brown water. Icy waves lapped at the hull coaxing him to get under way. The dock was dark and empty except for the pre-dawn shadows of lingering fish ghosts. He was the first to arrive.

At five o'clock sharp a freshly detailed Bentley wheeled into the parking lot. The car was immaculate, a 2009 Arnage RL Touring Sedan with gold trim, smoked windows, flawless black paint, even the wax had been waxed. Tobias had seen one other in his sixty-eight years. He knew the reputation of such an automobile. They had a price tag of 220 grand. This one, with all the bells and tweeters, would go 300 easy.

Tobias watched the sky begin to boil with anger. Lightning knifed through black clouds, stabbing at the water with sharp thrusts. A storm was brewing, a snaggle-toothed, razor-backed, blood-letting, she-dog of a storm. It was the kind of storm Tobias Kunkhe lived for.

The Bentley rolled to a stop, hogging two parking spaces. A man in his mid-forties slid out, turning his jacket collar up to ward off the morning chill. The Bentley door shut with a smooth, solid, two-grand thunk. The man approached with a confident swagger Tobias had seen before. It was a common trait among his clients. As he approached the dock, he paused to light a cigar, taking in the sweet smoke from a fresh Macanudo. Tobias was unfazed.

"You're the guy, right? The storm bringer?" His face was cloaked in shadow, but his voice was clear and forceful.

Tobias leaned heavy on the boat rail and hocked into the water again. "I been called that a time or six. You Rosselli?"

The man nodded, pacing the dock like he owned it. He extended his hand for the obligatory hand shake. Tobias gave him a quick up-and-down, ignoring his outstretched hand. "You bring it?"

Rosselli paused under the dock's lone security light, slid the sleek leather cigar case back in his jacket and nodded again. In the sparse light his features were revealed—forty-five and fit, close-cropped hair showing the first signs of gray. He was a man who commanded respect and usually got it.

"All of it?" Tobias asked.

"Absolutely."

Tobias watched Rosselli squirm. "Gonna need it up front, like we agreed."

Rosselli was pensive, grinding his fingernails into his palms with white-knuckle style. "Thought we might do a fifty-fifty. Half now and half when we're through."

Tobias breathed heavy into his callused palms. He grew weary of the last minute dickering. He could tell this one was far more accustomed to taking cash *in* than doling it *out*. "Get back in your car. We're done."

Rosselli's jaw dropped. "Hold up. No reason to get testy. I mean, we're just talking here, right? We're just two businessmen working out a little something-something, and *every* good businessman knows *everything* is negotiable, especially the price."

"Cough it up or pack it up, Rosselli. It's your choice. I got bigger fish to fry."

Rosselli wasn't used to compromise. He was a deal maker, the kind who always held all the right cards no matter how high the stakes. It was his forte'. "How about seventy five percent now and I hold the rest as security till we dock? Deal?"

Tobias turned and watched the storm draw closer, talking over his shoulder. "I don't do deals."

Rosselli took a long draw on the Macanudo, watching the tip glow like a devil's tail. When the smoke in his lungs expired, he released it into Tobias's face with a dismissive puff. "No reason we can't renegotiate, is there? Like I said, we're both businessmen, am I right?"

"The deal was eighty grand, Rosselli, up front, in cash, no exceptions.

Rosselli paused, then stepped back to the Bentley and popped the trunk. Tobias watched him fumble in the dark, keeping one hand on the .38 in his waistband in case Rosselli had the same idea.

Rosselli hoisted a canvas shoulder bag out of the trunk and brought it to Tobias. It was stuffed to the gills with neat stacks of hundreds—crisp, banded and unmarked. "It's all there. You can count it."

"I intend to."

Rosselli gave Tobias a half-hearted grin and climbed aboard the 'Stormy Weather'. "Let's hit it."

Tobias cut him short. "Not so fast. That's just half the bargain. Along with payment, you agreed to sign a waiver releasing me of all liability." He shoved a crumpled sheet of paper and a ball point pen into Rosselli's hands, eyeballing his manicured nails.

Rosselli scanned the document. "Sure-sure, but I assure you this won't be necessary. We have a gentleman's agreement that covers—"

"In return," Tobias interrupted, "I agree to take you into the eye of the biggest, black-toothed, motherfucker of a storm you've ever witnessed. While we're in the eye, you'll have a chance to catch the most gawdawful humongous fish you've ever ran into. You hook it, it's yours."

Rosselli tried to protest. Tobias held up a hand shushing him. "That's my rules. You don't wanna play by my rules, I could give a shit less. Won't be the first time someone punked-out on me. You agree to follow the rules, then sling some ink on that release and we cast off. Otherwise, the 'Stormy Weather' stays right where she's docked and you can cruise over to the yacht club, swill a half dozen double martinis, and talk to your pals about what could have been.

Lightning flashed over the glossy Black Bentley, making Rosselli cower like a beaten dog. He couldn't believe it. He'd been bested by a commoner, a bait and tackle boy. Still, he wanted bragging rights, something to puff up about while playing the back nine at Cedar Bluffs with the senior partners.

He grabbed the paper and signed it quick. It was the first time he'd signed anything without consent of his attorney.

Tobias looked at the signature, then folded the paper and shoved it in his pocket. He watched Rosselli, his arms crossed, foot tapping, eyes giving him that 'let's get on with it' look. Tobias marveled at his lack of preparation—the Italian loafers, tailored slacks, fitted shirt with French cuffs and starched collar. The man was totally clueless.

"We gonna do this thing or what?"

Tobias reached into a steamer trunk. "Not the best fishing gear you're wearing. You better put these on." He handed Rosselli a pair of knee-high rubber boots and some salt stained overalls.

Rosselli's nose wrinkled like he'd bit into a turd turnover. The boots were a size too small and the overalls smelled of chum and rancid fish guts. A white worm uncoiled and wriggled out of the pocket, hitting the deck with a soggy plop.

As they got under way, Rosselli opened a link and began yapping on his Bluetooth. Tobias marveled at the device hanging from Rosselli's ear like an eight gigabyte tumor. To Rosselli, it was his link to the outside world; to Tobias it was little more than a high priced, high-roller's security blanket. The first few miles were calm. Rosselli marveled at how smooth the 'Stormy Weather' cut through the water. The sky over the disappearing dock was as clear as a summer day. Sunlight gleamed off the gold trim of the Bentley sending out rays as bright as a lighthouse beacon. Up ahead was a different story. The clouds were gone. All that remained was a slate black sky stitched together with jagged threads of lightning.

As the storm began to rage, other boats blasted by on their way to dry land. Rosselli watched as other crews waved them off, pointing toward the shore with frantic hand gestures. Rosselli laughed into the wind, wondering how seasoned boatmen could turn tail so quickly in the face of a rain storm. Tobias stared straight ahead, steering toward deeper water. He pushed the throttle to full and took the building waves head-on.

Rosselli strained to get his sea legs. The sway of the boat worked on his gut like a bowl of sour chowder. He pulled a silver hip flask from his back pocket and unscrewed the cap.

"No drinking on deck," Tobias shouted from the helm.

Rosselli ignored the order and tipped the flask to his lips, drinking deeply. The bourbon cycloned down his throat and hit his stomach with an angry satisfying burn. He turned to face the storm, letting the rain pelt his neck and chest. Water rushed over the bow in white-lipped waves. At times the entire deck was momentarily submerged. A bolt of lightning struck an inch from Rosselli's left foot. He felt the raw current surge through his toes and shoot out his fingertips.

Tobias watched him from the wheelhouse. He'd seen it before. They came from every corner of the country, each of them dying to be weekend warriors, longing for the Great American Outdoor Adventure. They craved it like a junky shaking for a fix. Risk was their dope and men like Tobias became their suppliers. Tobias knew, at the first sign of real danger, most of them would roll up in a ball and shit themselves.

The waves continued to build, growing to twelve foot walls of angry brown water. With them, came driftwood, hanks of moss, dead limbs and roots, even wreckage from vessels too weak to survive previous storms. When the boat nosed in hard, Rosselli began to cower, confident the 'Stormy Weather' would capsize any second. Tobias cut the wheel hard, piercing the eye at a steep angle.

Deep inside the eye of the storm the water was as slick and smooth as greased glass. Tobias dropped anchor and pulled out a deck of cards. "I'll shuffle, you cut."

Rosselli looked at him in disbelief. "What the fuck? I came here to fish, not join a bridge club."

Tobias raked the cards through his fingers. "Gonna be about twenty minutes. My game is Tonk. Ever play it?"

"Hell no."

"You'll learn."

Rosselli emptied his hip flask in one final gulp. He cut the cards and waited for Tobias to deal. "Twenty minutes, no longer. After that I better be hauling in fish."

Tobias grinned and fanned the cards in his hand. "That's the thing about the great outdoors. You can't put a rush on nature."

Tobias and Rosselli played Tonk. Tobias won the better part of three hundred dollars while Rosselli wondered who in hell had contrived such a fucked up card game. Like clockwork, twenty minutes into the game Tobias gathered up the cards and his money and broke out the fishing gear.

"Hey, hold up here," Rosselli protested. Don't I get a chance to win my money back?"

Tobias let a smile leak across his lips. "You wanna fish or play cards?"

"Un-fuckin-believable, that's what you are."

Tobias checked the anchor and helped Rosselli prep his gear. Soon he was pulling in sea bass the size of dolphins. In less than an hour he filled a hundred gallon cooler, and the forward bait well. He had enough fish to feed the crew of the Lusitania. His arms burned from working the heavy rod and his manicured fingers were shredded with cuts and blisters.

"Had enough?" Tobias asked.

"Hell no! I paid for the full ride, I'm takin' the full ride."

Tobias watched the storm eye begin to close, bringing the storm back to life. He didn't have much time. "Better hang on then."

Rosselli's body was running on the high octane fuel of adrenaline. "I'm still waiting for that monster fish you promised." He paced the deck shaking his fist and shouting like an angry Baptist preacher speaking in tongues. "Most people can talk a good game, they just can't deliver. A deal's not a deal unless it delivers. So tell me Tobias, exactly where *is* this fish-to-beat-all-fish you talked so much about? Huh?"

Tobias tightened his grip, holding onto the wheel as if the boat might explode into splinters at any moment. "It's comin'."

The water around the 'Stormy Weather' began to churn into a foamy viscous stew of mossy limbs and oily scales. A stench crawled up Rosselli's nose and tickled the barf trigger in his brain. The contents of his freshly consumed flask spewed out and painted the deck around his toes oatmeal gray. Rosselli felt the line go taut. Three sharp tugs, then something hit the hook with such force it took the tips of two fingers before he had time to clear them from the spinning reel. Blood gushed forth in a geyser, soaking the rod and slickening the handle. Rosselli turned green. "What the hell is it?" he shouted, trying to maintain his grip on the bloody rod.

"That?" Tobias shouted, pointing to the rolling stench at the end of Rosselli's line. "Why that's your full ride."

The wind let out a howl—low, deep and animalistic. Rosselli could feel the strength draining from his arms, as if the thing on the end of his line was pulling him down the rod and dragging him into a simmering pot of steaming sewage. The line gave a final yank, then went slack. A bulbous head rose from the ocean. Eyes the size of basketballs glowed orange in their coal black sockets. Its body, black as midnight sin, ran the length of the 'Stormy Weather's' forty-two foot hull. The skin was alive with scales that left oily rainbows in the water. Rosselli turned to Tobias Kunkhe, searching his eyes, hoping for any explanation of what was happening to him. The wicked grin on Tobias's face told him he wouldn't be getting one.

The creature rose out of the water in one slow, smooth motion. Its face was a mass of mossy scales and warts. Gill slits like ragged axe wounds expanded and collapsed with each rasping breath. It moved in close, inches from Roselli's face. The stench rolled over him in half-pipe waves. His knees buckled. He felt hot slobbering breath at the back of his neck, breath that smelled like a moldy burlap sack full of rotting venison.

Tobias patted the creature's slippery lip. It let out a slow whistling grunt. "Mr. Rosselli, this is Ol' Lloyd. Lloyd, this is lunch." The creature extended a long pair of spines from its dorsal fin. They lashed out with the force of a rifle shot, impaling Rosselli's neck. He stood motionless on the deck, paralyzed with fear and the poisonous venom now pumping into his blood stream.

"You see," said Tobias, "me and Ol' Lloyd, we've got a— what was it you called it? Ah yes, a gentleman's agreement. I keep him fed and in return he lets me catch all the fish I want."

The creature's rubbery lips parted, revealing a cavernous mouth full of barbed teeth. They drew inward with each new clack of its powerful jaws. It sniffed Rosselli slowly and carefully, like a dog whiffing a mate's ass. Rosselli opened his mouth to scream. The creature opened wider, letting out a hideous unearthly wail. Rosselli was devoured in one vicious snap. All that remained was a bloody forearm flopping on the deck.

Tobias slipped the Rolex off Rosselli's severed arm and kicked the bloody stump overboard. As it disappeared into the churning vortex, he went to his quarters and added the watch to his collection. It was a nice piece. That new fishing trawler was one step closer to being his. He'd have to sink the Bentley. It was too easy to trace. Besides, what self-respecting fisherman would drive such a thing? Leather seats and burlwood trim weren't exactly his mug of grog. Now an F150 with a power winch? *That* was a vehicle.

Tobias hoisted anchor at the same instant a stunning brunette appeared from the cabin below. She walked with an elegance that made men drive cars head-on into utility poles.

"Mrs. Rosselli. I wondered how long you were going to stay below. You've gone and missed all the excitement."

The brunette pulled a French rolled cigarette from a gold case and got it going with her monogrammed lighter. Her voice was an octave lower than one would expect from a woman of her build. "Is he—? I mean did he—?"

"Yep."

She took a long drag from the cigarette, letting the smoke entertain her lungs for a full thirty seconds before releasing it through her nostrils. "Marvelous. You are a man of your word."

"All that's left is to settle up," Tobias said. "You did bring the cash right?"

She placed a foot on the rail, eyeing a run in her stocking. The soft material of her skirt hugged the lines of her body. "Of course I brought it. After all, that was the agreement."

Tobias secured the dripping anchor and fired the engine. He pictured her long creamy-white legs, alive under the silky material. If her skirt were any shorter it could be a scarf. His head swam.

"I have to hand it to you, those smelly overalls masked my perfume perfectly, just like you said. He was so busy retching he never suspected a thing." She moved in closer, sliding an arm around Tobias's waist. "Now about your fee."

Tobias eyed the leather case in her hand. "A hundred grand, all cash, all now."

"Got it right here sweetie." She ran her slender fingers over the smooth leather case. "I was wondering," she cooed. "Could we maybe work out a deal?" Her free hand gently rubbed his stomach just above the belt line.

Tobias turned and hugged her close, filling his lungs with her floral scent. Then, he shoved her overboard. "I don't do deals."

The water percolated into a rolling boil, turning in on itself in thick foaming curls. The eye of the storm had closed. The sky opened up, vomiting torrents of rain that skipped over the water like liquid arrows. It stung Tobias's face and burned his eyes. He smiled and hit the throttle. The 'Stormy Weather' responded with a powerful drone. Tobias put the storm to his back and steered toward the shoreline. First thing in the morning he'd call the Marina. Maybe see if he could work a deal on that seventy-two footer they'd just rebuilt. It was a killer fishing boat.

LONELY AFTER DARK

Tim Curran

There were a lot of crazy old wives tales floating around Sawyer County. One of them was that you didn't go out on Spider Lake after dark, not in the dead of winter, but that particular January night we decided to ignore what old wives said and it was the worst mistake of our lives.

We were sitting in Dutch Shulman's ice shanty jigging for pike, listening to the wind screaming across the frozen lake. A blizzard was coming in, blown down from Lake Superior and pushing darkness before it, but the fish were biting and already Dutch had laid in a mess of jumbo perch and a pair of walleye on wigglers and waxworms. I was jigging for pike using a spoon and a hunk of chicken skin. I had taken a nice thirty-six incher, but I knew there were bigger ones down there, hunting through the weed beds on the shoal beneath us.

As things stood, we weren't about to call it a day. Not after six hours on the ice. Things were getting good now.

"Funny how it goes, Fife," Dutch said, hooking a wiggler and dropping it into a hole in the ice, feeding it down deep and feeling for bottom, taking up the slack on the ceiling rig. "You sit on yer ass half a day and you ain't gettin' squat, then *boom*, you can't get your lines in the water fast enough."

"Ain't it the truth," I said, trying not to double-over with the sudden pain that was chewing at my vitals.

Dutch's shack was roomy. Eight foot by ten, benches to either side, six holes augered down through the ice, all of them eighteen inches so you had to watch where you walked. We'd spent most of the day drinking beer, yarning, skimming ice off the holes, and roasting hot dogs in the woodstove, and now the fishing had begun. The blizzard was getting randy out there, making the shack tremble from time to time as if it had been shaken by a fist. The snow beating against the door sounded like blowing sand.

My bladder was full up, so I stepped outside for a leak and the snow was flying heavy, the wind cutting right through me. Shadows lay thick over the drift making me feel uneasy, but I shook it off, finished my business, and went back inside.

"Getting dark out there," I told Dutch, pulling off a cigarette, watching the smoke twist and turn in the yellow glare of the lanterns.

"Yup. Blizzarding, too. You want to call her a day, start fresh in the A.M.?"

"No, fish are running, let's run with 'em."

Dutch liked that idea fine and I could see it on his face. Yet deep inside me, there was a sense of doom that made my old blood run like ice water, made me feel the storm blowing out there and the darkness itself closing in.

After all, we were over a mile out on Spider Lake.

And the sun had gone down.

Dutch worked his lines and I kept an eye on my tip-ups. Now and again, he would cast a look in my direction and what I saw in his eyes was part anxiety and part mischievousness. Anxiety, probably, because we had good reason to be off the ice before nightfall and mischievousness because there was a certain thrill in what we were doing, like a couple kids breaking curfew for a midnight visit to the local haunted house. I felt it too. And despite the fact I was a few years short of seventy, it made me feel almost giddy, really alive for the first time in years. It was a dare, I suppose, and we were taking it on. With the pains coming and going in my gut, I figured I was nearly out of dares so I had to take 'em where I could get 'em.

It wasn't five minutes later when something thumped against the outside of the shack making us both jump. It made my old ticker skip a beat.

Then the door swung open, snow and wind blowing through, the gas lanterns swinging back and forth on their hooks. Some guy came stumbling in, scaring the hell out of us, blood splashed over his parka in crazy whorls. I figured it wasn't his monthly so I knew we were in for it.

He went down on his hands and knees, breathing hard. "There's something under the goddamn ice," he said, just half out of his mind with panic. "Something down there! It came up out of the hole! It grabbed Al...*it grabbed him and he was screaming, blood flying...oh Jesus Christ...*"

I looked over at Dutch and he looked at me.

"Shut the damn door," he said, getting out his bottle of medicinal Jack Daniels and giving our visitor a few pulls off it while he babbled on, making little sense. The whiskey took the edge off, but he was still in some kind of state. His name was Mike Modek, he said, and he was an architect from Madison. He'd come to Spider Lake with his brother, Al, to do a little ice fishing. It was a getaway they'd been planning for months after Al had visited the Spider—as we locals called it—and caught his limit during walleye season. Sure and fine. Then not twenty minutes ago something had happened, something unbelievable and gruesome.

I had forgotten about the fish by then. I was seeing all that blood on Modek's parka, drops of it spattered across his pale face. There were things I could have said to him then, things that would have either curled the hairs at the back of his neck or got him to thinking that I was not only old but crazy. I kept my mouth shut.

"Tell us again, Mr. Modek," Dutch said, feeding another pine split into the woodstove. "Just take it easy and tell us exactly what you saw."

Modek breathed in and out, his eyes bright with fear, the muscles of his face bunching like they were tied in knots just beneath the skin. "We were at the shack," he said, his voice breaking high and low, "and I was just sitting there, you know, listening to Al. He...he starts talking, Christ, he won't let you go...twenty minutes of bullshit about jigging with Swedish Pimples...and then something grabbed Al's line, it snapped it right off the rig...he reached down into the hole to get his bobber because it was still floating and something fucking *grabs* him...starts pulling him down..."

"What? What was it?"

But Modek just shook his head. "Something white...something fast...it took hold of him, it yanked him down..."

Dutch got it out of him by degrees. He couldn't say what it was, but it had come up and taken hold of his brother and pulled him down the hole which was insane to begin with, he admitted to us. The holes Al had drilled through the ice were no more than twelve inches in diameter and Al went in at nearly 300 pounds...it would have been like trying to drag an oak stump through a mouse hole.

But something, apparently, had managed it just fine.

"He kinda...he kinda *exploded*," Modek said, a sour-stinking sweat breaking open on his face. "Blew up."

I sat there listening like a kid hearing a campfire tale of a ghost looking for its head in the forest. It was crazy. Absolutely crazy. There was nothing under the ice but fish. And no fish was big enough in Spider Lake to take hold of a man let alone smash him into something that might *fit* down a hole a foot in diameter. But the blood...there was no getting around that.

The shack shook as the howling wind out there picked up, making a distant, lonesome sound. I was hearing something on it. Something that left me cold. It was a mournful sort of moaning, rising and falling, filled with anguish. It had an almost female caliber to it. Then it was gone.

I kept telling myself it was imagination, only I knew better.

Modek stayed there on his knees, shivering despite the warmth coming off the stove. He looked like he maybe wanted to pray and under the circumstances that might have been a good idea. "Tried my cell, tried 911, but all I got was static. I'm getting four bars, I should be getting through."

He dug it out of his pocket and handed it to me. I was no expert, but it appeared to be working just fine. I punched in 911 and put the phone to my ear with a hand that trembled. There was some crackling static on the other end, but mostly an empty, listening silence. The sort of sound you might have heard putting your ear up to the wall of a deserted house: a sound not unlike a hushed respiration.

As chills crawled up my spine and down my arms, I was almost certain someone was on the other end, breathing.

I snapped it closed and handed it back to him.

"Things get funny on the Spider come winter," was all I said.

He just stared at me, maybe writing me off then and there as some crazy old coot.

"You're out in the boonies here, Mr. Modek," Dutch told him. "Nobody gets a signal out on the Spider. Especially not in the winter time. It's an...an atmospheric thing."

"What the hell are you talking about?"

"What I'm talking about, son, is that you should have been off the ice by dark. Things happen out on the Spider come sundown. Things that no stranger like you could know about."

Modek just kneeled there on the ice, his face hooked somewhere between a scowl and a laugh. Just a couple hayseeds. That's what he was thinking and maybe he was right and maybe he was dangerously wrong. He was city-born and city-bred. I'm not going to say that automatically makes him a fool, all I'm saying is that it takes more than fancy mail-order Gel Lite gloves, polar fleece, and a shiny new L. L. Bean parka to know the ice, to feel its promise and its threat. It's something you're born to.

"What kinda goddamn fish you got around here," he breathed. "What kinda thing was—"

"Weren't no fish, Mr. Modek," Dutch told him, pulling out his 12-guage Marlin from the wooden box under his seat, breaking it open and pumping a few shells into the breech.

I said, "You think it was—"

Dutch nodded. "What else could it possibly be?"

Modek looked from me to Dutch and back at me again. "Will one of you kindly tell me what the hell you're talking about, goddammit? My brother...*my brother is fucking dead*...and I think I have the right to know what this is about!"

"No," Dutch told him, "you don't have the right to shit, Mr. Modek. Because I'm willing to bet that in town they told you to get off the ice before dark. Maybe they said it was because of blizzards or squalls or whiteouts or what not. But I *know* they told you and I also know you were too damn stupid to listen to them."

"You have no right to talk to me like that—"

"Shut your pisshole," I told him. "You've put all our lives in danger now. So have the decency to shut up."

Poor Modek. Here he came for a bit of relaxation with his brother, something to relieve the stress of his corporate life, maybe a nagging high-born wife or a pack of demanding kids...and he gets this.

Believe me, I wanted to tell him then. I wanted to tell him all about Spider Lake. How it had always been a damn good place to catch your limit, maybe do some swimming or boating in the July sunshine. But come winter, when the ice showed and the wind came blowing and the snow drifted, it could be a bad place. Especially after dark. That's what I wanted to say. But if I told him that, then I'd have to tell him the rest about people disappearing out on the ice come winter, always after sundown. And he would not have liked that part. It had been going on since 1953, you see, because that was the year a crazy drunken fool name of Bones Pilon had gotten some crazy idea in his head about driving across the Spider in his old man's pick-up before the ice had set—first week of December, it was. Well, the truck went through, sinking like a brick into the deepest part of the lake, some three hundred fifty feet straight down. Bones swam out, made it back to town like some walking ice sculpture...but his girlfriend, Gina Shiner, had not. They never did recover her body and to my knowledge, Bones' pick-up is still down there in the mud and silt rotting away like a buried coffin.

I was ten years old at the time and it was a real tragedy.

I knew Gina on account my ma used her as a babysitter for us kids when she was off working at the linen mill, midnights, in Edgewater after my old man got hit by the Chicago-Northwestern special delivery and they had to take his remains off the tracks in bags and buckets. Gina was great and we all loved her.

Then she went through the ice.

And we all knew and hated the asshole responsible. When he ate the gun not a year later, nobody shed a tear.

Back in 'fifty-three, Bones, and his brother Stipp—who brewed his own whiskey and lost an eye in a knife fight—lived together in a tar paper shack on Swanson Creek out in the Big Piney Woods. No electricity. They were good with engines, those boys, good with poaching, bad with holding jobs and keeping out of jail. What Gina had been doing with a guy like Bones was anyone's guess, but truth be told she always did have a wild streak in her and a true lack of judgment.

Anyway, after that business, people started disappearing out on Spider Lake in those dark months between December's first real freeze and April's true thaw. I knew of five men myself that vanished before 1960. They said sometimes they didn't disappear completely, maybe leaving a little—or a lot—of blood behind, but never anything else. Maybe that was fiction. I don't know. The sheriff went through a cursory investigation every time, but never turned up anything. And the surviving widows or mothers or fathers knew better than to push him on it. They got real good at making up stories about how their missing kin had skipped town for one reason or another. And sometimes, hearing them tell it, it seemed like they almost *believed* their own lies. Maybe they *needed* to so they could sleep at night. But it was always there in their eyes—a haunted, terrified look that spoke volumes.

Bottom line: after a time locals knew better than to go out on the Spider at dead winter when the shadows grew long. When people turned up missing out there it was usually out-of-towners like our fine Mr. Modek and his brother.

"We can't just sit here!" Modek said, piping up again.

"We ain't gonna," I said, grabbing a flashlight.

Dutch pulled on his hat with the ear flaps. "Blizzard's kicking up its heels and it's dark out there. Let's go see what this is about."

Modek's shack was maybe two hundred feet away and it should have been a quick little jog, but the blizzard had descended with full fury, snow flying in white raging sheets. The wind was whipping and throwing drift around in twisting snow-devils and scooping up a fine scrim of ice particles that bit into our exposed faces like steel needles. The beam of my light made it maybe ten feet before reflecting back at us.

Dutch in the lead, we leaned into the blow, fighting against it. Now and again, the wind would lift and you could see all the shadowy boxes of ice shacks spread around on the frozen crust of Spider Lake, then it would come roaring back at near-whiteout conditions and visibility would be down to eight or ten feet at the outside.

I was getting hit by pains in my stomach again and I did everything I could so no one would notice.

My belly had been acting up for weeks by then and sometimes the pain got so bad, so deep, it would put me down to my knees and squeeze the tears from my eyes. I passed blood near every morning and now and again I'd spit up a clot in the dead of night, a coppery-tasting foul wad that would leave me shaking. Time to go to the doc? Oh, certainly. But like all old men, I put it off, unwilling to face the coming pall of the grave, hoping to keep it at arm's length as long as possible, wanting to know one more warm wheat-grassed July and one last bloom of September color before I turned toes up. To the old, you see, docs are undertakers and nothing more.

I walked with Modek next to me, so close we were practically holding hands. I don't think I've ever seen anyone so frightened in my life and the closer we got to the shack the more certain I was that there was a good reason for it.

Before she passed, my Gloria liked to tell me that I was not the most sensitive of individuals, but that night my sensitivity, my empathy, was alive and electric inside me. I was feeling the black depths of Modek's trauma right to my marrow, but I was feeling more than that. Something else I couldn't quite put a finger on, something dark and hungry gathering around us, circling like slat-thin wolves.

"Why are we doing this?" Modek said to me. "Shouldn't...shouldn't we just go get the sheriff or state police? Let them handle this?"

"Let's just take a look," I said.

The shack suddenly appeared out of the gloom and to a man, we stopped dead there in the snow and wind, staring at it like it was an open casket. I panned it with my light. The wind had piled drifts up around it, the door slamming back and forth against its frame.

Modek was wired tight, ready to bolt. I was ready to do the same, truth be told. As I watched the door banging open and closed, I was very much aware of a feeling at the back of my neck that had absolutely nothing to do with the cold pushing down into the single digits. The storm was howling around us like some primal beast, the wind and whipping snow creating weird jumping shadows over the ice.

Dutch took hold of the door.

In the beam of the flashlight I clearly saw five ragged ruts torn into it like the trails of claws.

It was a little two-man shack, cramped benches to either side, holes augered through the ice, a little gas stove. Not much bigger than your average outhouse, truth be told. Just your ordinary ice shack... except it looked like it had been dipped in red ink.

Blood was sprayed up the walls in frozen spirals and hanging from the ceiling in red icicles. The ice was stained crimson, a clotted sea of blood and bits of tissue and iced flesh. What might have been an ear was frosted right to the wall in a trail of ichor.

That was all bad enough, but worse was written in there on the wall in bloody letters in a childlike scrawl:

BONES

BONES

BONES

"Jesus," Dutch said, pulling away from the doorway.

Modek was having trouble breathing, just gasping for air. "What does that mean?" he asked. "*What the hell does that mean?*"

But neither Dutch or I answered him. We just stood around, not looking at each other. Shadows were spreading over the ice like long, reaching fingers.

I leaned against the shack because I had a sudden need of something solid behind me as my belly began to roll with fingers of pain. Like rivers branching into creeks and streams, it spread out from my lower belly and reached up into my chest in a tightening basket of agony, red-hot and sharp. It brought tears to my eyes.

"You okay, Fife?" Dutch asked me and I nodded.

Modek and his brother had come out on the ice in a shiny new Polaris snowmobile. It was parked out behind the shack. The hood had been nearly torn off. The engine looked like somebody had taken a sledgehammer after it... coils and hoses were hanging out like spilled guts, dark fluids gushed into the snow.

"My sled!" Modek cried. "Look what they did to my sled!"

"Mr. Modek—" I started to say.

But he shoved me aside and hooked Dutch's arm, started shouting, "WHAT THE HELL IS THIS ALL ABOUT? YOU FUCKING BOTH KNOW AND I WANT YOU TO TELL ME RIGHT GODDAMN NOW!"

He was like some wild thing that had finally been uncaged, eyes bright and dangerous, face pulled into a sneer of animal hate. Dutch might have been near on seventy, but he was strong as a bull. He tossed Modek aside and Modek slipped on the ice and went down on his ass. In his frustration and anger, he began to shake and make a pathetic whimpering sound.

I helped him to his feet and before I could stop myself, I was telling him what I figured he had a right to know. "It's a ghost, Mr. Modek," I said, my chest pinching tight. "That's what this is about. There's a ghost out here. Some years ago a woman went through the ice and never found her way back out. Part of her is still down there. It comes out during the winter months after dark."

"A ghost," he said like it was a word he had never expected to use. "A ghost."

"I know how it sounds but it's the best I can do," I told him. "Whatever it is... maybe all the bad things we leave behind us when we die unexpectedly... it's still down there. And it's filled with hate."

He backed away from me, uttering a bitter, sarcastic laugh. "A ghost? You're a goddamn nutcase, you know that? You ought to be committed. Both of you ought to be committed."

Dutch turned away from him and led me off into the storm. "Well, you tried. Leave it at that."

"Where do you think you're going?" Modek said behind us.

"We're going back to the shack," Dutch said. "You can do any goddamn thing you want, Modek. It's no sweat off my ass."

"But these other shacks... shouldn't we get some help—"

"Nobody in 'em. Not after dark."

Modek fell in behind us as we began the slow—and for old men like us *painful*—crawl back to Dutch's shack. He was ranting and raving, threatening lawsuits and police intervention and you name it, but he stuck close to us like a babe frightened to be separated from its mother.

Dutch and I kept our yaps shut. All we cared about at that moment was reaching the safety of the shack before that wind got too far deep inside us and frosted us white, seized up our old carcasses and planted 'em deep in the drift like a couple stringy chops on ice. We needed warmth. We need a cup of something hot. The wind continued to blow and the snow was not light and fluffy like you see on Christmas cards and TV shows, but fine and biting and abrasive, driven by that wind so it scratched your face raw... what you could feel of your face, that was, in that godawful cold sweeping down from the big lake.

I steered a path for us with my light, but in those near-whiteout conditions we were going more by instinct than anything else. The sky was a boiling maelstrom of white threaded with pink like it gets when the worst storms blow and you could not truly see any dividing line between it and the ice itself. Drifts were forever forming, disintegrating, and building back up like frozen white waves. Our tracks were already nearly gone.

We marched along, each of us feeling the cold in our hearts and much of that had to do with the damnably bleak situation we were in. I knew Dutch was thinking about his pickup truck, wondering if it had been gotten to as well. Because if it had, we were trapped, you see.

Spider Lake sat out in federal forest land, five miles from the nearest town which was Cobton. Nothing but a Boy Scout camp on the eastern shore, a few fishing lodges and summer cabins. At five miles long and nearly four in width, it was sizeable for an inland lake but just a puddle compared to the big lake of Superior. We were a good mile and a half out on it in a blizzard. If we had to walk for shore, I figured they'd find us curled up in a snowdrift come morning. My joints would never hold up, not with the wind biting at them.

It seemed that after a time the flashlight weighed about as much as a cinder block. My back was aching, my knees feeling hot and numb, legs cold and stiff, belly rumbling with a distant memory of pain. The wind never stopped, of course. If anything it got meaner, blowing with an angry screeching at times and a low, mournful howling at others. I began to think I was hearing voices on it... whispering voices calling out to me, calling my name, beckoning me off into the storm.

The wind gets funny in a blizzard, though, and you can imagine all kinds of things.

We weren't far from the shack, I figured, when out of the storm came something that was no wind: a high-pitched, weird braying that came and went, each time getting closer and closer until it was so loud that it was nearly ear-splitting.

"What the hell is that?" Modek said. "Is it... is it some kind of animal?"

I didn't answer because I'd already told him what was out there and because I could not seem to find my voice. We had stopped and maybe that wasn't such a hot idea, but in the storm we couldn't be sure where that awful noise was coming from and, believe me, we weren't comfortable with that. The snow blew heavy around us, sheets of drift spraying us white. In the glow of the flashlight Dutch was looking at me with bright, glistening eyes, his facial muscles frozen in a grim half-smile as if they would not relax.

We listened to that braying voice cutting through the storm, every time inches closer, the very tone of it shrieking and inhuman like the cry of baboons.

"Dutch," I said. "I think it's—"

"Shhh!"

He was listening for something and then I was too and it was like being out in the woods in autumn, listening for the tread of game only this time *we* were the game. I heard a soft crunching of footsteps coming through the snow in our direction. They were slow and methodical but definitely coming out of the storm at us.

And then Modek screamed, "I SEE IT! IT'S OVER THERE! I SEE IT!"

I don't know what he saw, but I put the flashlight in that direction and I saw a shape... a distorted shape like a moving sack pulling back into the shadows. It had eyes. Bright yellow eyes.

The terror inside me was hot and cutting, filling my chest with live wires. I couldn't move. I couldn't do anything but wait for it to find me.

"Enough," Dutch said. "C'mon! Let's go! Move it! We have to get back to the shack..."

The braying was gone and we no longer heard the footfalls. There was only a hushed, waiting silence out there. Even the wind had gone quiet as if it, too, was listening. We started marching again and we hadn't gone very far at all when a voice came out of the shadows. It was a woman's voice: darkly sweet and cold as the ice we stood on, scratching like rats in narrow walls. "Bones?" it said. "Bones... are you there?"

My heart about stopped. I wheeled around with the light, not sure what I was going to see. The snow blew around us and we were in whiteout conditions. Whatever was out there could have been ten feet away and we wouldn't have seen it.

"Bones?"

The voice was behind us.

"Bones?"

It was in front of us.

"Bones?"

To the left, to the right, coming at us from every direction with a cold hissing sibilance that nearly put me to my knees. Modek was making a whimpering sound and Dutch was aiming his shotgun in every which direction only there was nothing to shoot at, only a voice that drew in closer and closer and then—

I think Modek screamed. It was a high, girlish sound of absolute fright. Dutch said something... and then... and then I heard a flapping sort of sound like sheets on a line or the high shrouds of a schooner in a good blow and a white, blurred, long-armed shape came wheeling, drifting out of the blizzard. I saw a waxen, moon-pallid face like that of a bleached, fish-chewed corpse rising from the deeps. And long talons like those of a beast streaking right at Dutch's face. He cried out as they ripped across his eyes, blinding him as they slit deep and scraped across the bone beneath.

Then he was down on his knees, gripping his face, blood spraying in the snow and it came again:

"Bones? Bones?"

That evil, distorted thing came out of the darkness so fast I couldn't properly track it with my eyes. When it again pulled back, Dutch's throat was torn open and his face was nearly peeled from the skull below. When I threw off Modek, clinging to me like a squalling brat, Dutch was dead, his blood staining the snow red. Sprays of it were scattered in every direction and I saw a trail of it leading off into the darkness.

I heard a shrill, hysterical cackling that faded off into the dark belly of the storm.

I grabbed Modek who was blubbering like a spoiled kid, dragging him through the snow with a strength I had not felt in my old bones in many years. I pulled him along, making for the shack and hoping beyond hope we were still moving in its direction and not towards some dead thing waiting out in the storm for us. The wind rose and fell in cycles with jangling, discordant notes like some far-off calliope gone somber and hollow.

The shack.

Not far, not far at all and my instinctive, internal pilot told me we were closing in on it. The wind was doing everything it could to push us back, rising up and blowing snow around us in eddies and whirls. Then, just when I was daring to breathe, a voice came cycling at us out of the blizzard—scratching, shrill, female. It went right up my spine and nestled at the back of my neck like icy pins.

"Bones... Bones, I'm coming..."

Female, *yes*, but not a woman...not really, maybe the twisted anti-human memory of one...the voice of some soulless thing *mocking* the voice of a woman. I felt a current of electricity go thrumming through my bones.

I saw eyes coming at us... like open, infected wounds.

The shack. We were only five feet away and then the voice came again: *"Bones... is that you?"*

I threw Modek through the door and he stumbled, knee going down into one of the holes in the ice. I sensed movement behind me, heard that flapping sound again like a blowing sheet, and pulled the door closed. And as I did, mere inches from being shut, something pulled at it from the other side and black, thorny nails slid around the edge tearing into the wood. Then I slammed it shut and threw the latch in place. It wasn't much in the way of a lock but it was all we had.

But what was out there wasn't done yet.

There was a scratching sound like fingernails being dragged over the walls and that godawful, hideous voice calling out for *Bones*. It was like the whining, mewling voice of a cat in the dead of night sounding almost human but not quite.

By that point, my mind was like a churning pulp of terror. The pains in my stomach came in waves, aches threading through my limbs. I fell onto one of the benches, gasping, shivering, but knowing I had to keep it together because Modek looked like he was in shock. He was just kneeling on the ice, rocking back and forth, mumbling incoherently under his breath. He had the glassy, bovine eyes of a stunned cow.

I fed a few logs into the woodstove to get some warmth into us and that's when what was out there began clawing at the door with a manic, wild sort of frenzy. Soon, the entire shack was shaking. The lanterns overhead were swinging back and forth and I clearly smelled the hot stink of Modek's shit as he fouled himself.

And that voice... constant, perpetual, agonized and evil but with a bone-deep despair feeding through it: *"Bones... Bones... let me in... please let me in... Booooonnnes... Booooonnnnnes... let me in..."* It was the high and keening voice of a hag scraping on a dry wind.

"GO AWAY, GINA!" I shouted. "DEAR GOD, GO AWAY!"

And somehow, someway, that seemed to work. The shack stopped trembling. The voice was gone. There was nothing out there but the whistle of the wind, snow brushing against the walls. The perpetual creaking and cracking of the ice you hear on cold, cold nights.

I found Dutch's medicinal bottle and pulled hard off it. I got a cigarette into my mouth with both hands and drew deep, wondering what in God's name I was going to do. Modek was dead silent, that shiny and shell-shocked look in his eyes. If we struck out on foot and he cracked up and ran off, there was no way at my age I would be able to stop him. Dutch's pickup was out there, but I had a nasty feeling that Gina had seen to that, too. Whatever she had been as a girl, she was no longer. This thing was just a revenant, a shadow, a malefic memory. I knew Gina. She was spiteful and you didn't want to piss her off, but down deep she was good and she was kind. That's who she had been.

But what about at the point of death?

What was she then?

What would any of us be as we were trapped in a sinking truck, locked in an iron coffin? Angry? Terrified? Hateful, even? Certainly. Maybe that's what ghosts are—the earthbound instincts and animal drives, the need to survive coupled with all the awful, squirming things of the human condition: hunger, hate, violence, greed, madness. No mercy or charity or love. Those things pass on with the soul, what's left behind is the psychic energy of those last moments, eternal and undying, energized into a wraith or a shade, a hungering, hating force of vengeance. They say energy can't be destroyed it can only change shape—and maybe that's exactly what it does.

I sat there, ruminating for maybe ten or fifteen minutes, trying not to listen to Modek's whining little boy voice, and then something began to happen. The ice began to creak and shift beneath us and something like a hot steam came from the holes at our feet. The water and slush bubbled in them. I saw a face looking up at me from the one nearest my boot. It was distorted like running tallow cooling on a skull. I saw wormholed eyes staring up at me and then... *she rose.*

I can't properly explain how she came up through that hole, but she did, something elastic and rubbery, moist and ectoplasmic, fluid and oozing... she rose up, white and puckered, slicked with mud from the bottom and strung with rotting lake weed like garland. The stink she brought with her was sickening. It was up my nose. It made my eyes water. It filled my mouth with a taste of putrescence like biting into a rotten apple, filled with wormy mush and crawling flies.

She had been down there a long, long time.

Now she came up in a hissing helix of ice-fog—hair like twisted black roots growing from white bone, face nothing but crawling moon-white pulp shot through with tiny holes from the things that had been burrowing into her. There was a crooked, wicked grin on that face like the cut of a scythe and depthless slate-black eyes like windows looking down into the blackest charnel hell I could imagine. Anything remotely human or good had been milked from her.

She was living, festering, animate hunger.

She opened her mouth, pitted lips pulling away from tar-black gums and a scream came spraying out of her like vomit and it must have been the very scream Gina Shiner had let loose right before the black waters entombed her in Bones' pickup truck on the bottom.

She began to shudder and shake, moving with frantic, stiff whiplike motions of her limbs, her head snapping back and forth on her neck. Moving faster and faster like some gyrating dancer in a strobe light, an obscene puppet with jerking strings.

I heard Modek scream like he was being flayed as she took hold of him, shrieking the name of her lover in his face.

The lanterns overhead both went out.

By then I had thrown myself out the door and scrambled away across the snow, madly climbing hills of shattered ice that rose from the pack like the broken prows of ghost ships. That's when I turned back, just as the blizzard played out some and a thin, sickly moonlight spilled over the ice. Somehow, Modek had gotten away. He was moving through the drifts with the scuttling motion of a beach crab. He saw Dutch's pickup truck. He threw himself at it, yanked the door open, and climbed inside. The keys were in it and he got it going. The headlights came on.

But he was not alone.

The ghost was suckered to the windshield like some human fly, a writhing, flapping thing that seemed to be fragmenting and breaking apart in the wind.

I saw the truck vibrating. I heard ice cracking and the gushing, roar of water as it rushed up from below and the pickup slid back off a sheet of pack into the fuming lake. The front end bobbed for a moment or two like the bow of a ship, then down it went with a gurgling sound. Beneath the dark waters, the headlights gradually faded away, finally winking out like eyes closing. Then the ice slid back in place, crashing and booming, and all was quiet.

My memory gets a bit vague at that point. All I can say for sure is I started walking towards the shore and whether that took two hours or six I cannot say. Sometimes it comes back to me in my dreams... the screech of the wind, the blowing snow, the shadows jumping across the ice, and the voices of the dead calling to me out of the night and the storm and some shattered gray corridor of hell caught in-between.

I think Gina followed me.

I have certain delirious, deranged memories of hearing her calling out for Bones and the sound of it still rings in my ears as if she were right next to me when she cried his name. I can only be sure that two or three times I heard the sound of feet following me and saw eyes yellow as autumn moons peering out at me through the snowstorm.

Maybe I imagined it. I don't know.

But the closer I *did* get to shore—and I could feel the reach of it extending a hand to me—the farther away was the voice of the thing that had been Gina Shiner: some dim and phobic memory, an unholy will to survive. A ghost haunting the bones of its former existence, reliving those last tormented moments again and again. As that voice faded into the storm and I was distanced from it, I could finally hear the absolute despair and loneliness of it, the melancholy, pitiful cry of something lost in a black dimension of horror, forever trying to find its way out of the darkness and into the light, reaching out for the hand of Bones Pilon which it would never, ever find.

They found me on the county trunk road towards morning. I spent a month in the hospital for exposure, exhaustion, and frostbite. I lost two toes and the pinkie on my left hand. While I was there, they discovered several tumors in my gut which came as no surprise to me. I evaded death that night only to find it still had a solid grip on me. They operated, of course, but it only spread and they gave me two months at the outside.

I survived an encounter with that thing on the ice. I lost my best friend in the world and buried a good part of my soul out there.

Now, as I lay in my hospital bed, the ticking of the deathwatch beetle getting louder in my ears and my time growing short, I worry on things. I worry on things undone and unsaid, crushed hopes and wasted dreams, desires unfulfilled and longings unsatisfied. The shadows and impulses that might live after us, forever lonesome, forever hungering. I think about the good things we take with us and the starving evil we leave behind and what form it might take. And if some of that might still be out on the Spider, waiting for dark to come.

FERRY-MOANS

J.M. Harris

It has always been my private conviction that any man who pits his intelligence against a fish and loses has it coming. ~ John Steinbeck

Ryan first saw the girl crouching in the reeds. Beside him, the Amazon snaked its way deeper into the forest, its hollows filling and then emptying in lapping gulps. His surroundings had been muted by the whispered lullaby of the water, but the girl awakened a primal instinct, and his senses tuned in, the pulse of insect chatter loud, the warble of exotic bird song chaotic. The girl appeared feral, her movements visceral and quick. As she rose up, a memory hit him in a series of snapshots, and a blazing summer three decades previous came back as clear and vibrant as the sky above him.

***

Ryan sat beside his ten-speed, a stalking rod resting across his knees. Having experimented with several lures with no luck, he secured a Silver Wriggler to the end of his line; he hoped it would tempt a brown trout from the shadow-dappled margins on the far bank.

It was hot, so hot his twelve year old skin had never tanned to the point of golden before. He'd never burned either, and picked at a dry piece of skin on his nose, leaving a pink tender patch underneath—he didn't know it, but these mundane details would come back with the same startling clarity as the girl who approached him through the veil of hay dust and pollen that day.

She was older (the bumps under the T shirt she'd knotted up above her pale midriff told him that much), and her hair flowed long, thick and red. Freckles dusted a scarlet ribbon of skin banding her cheeks and nose. Her teeth were large and square. She wasn't particularly pretty, but her smile and confident approach stole the breath from his lungs, scared him the way only pre-pubescent boys could be frightened at the prospect of talking to an older girl.

"Caught much?" she said, beaming, hand on hip.

He shook his head, and to his dismay, she laughed and stepped closer. "Well, I know the secret to catching big fish."

Ryan wanted to scowl and tell her to get lost, only managing to raise his eyebrows.

"Don't talk much, do you?"

He shrugged, "What's this secret, then?"

"Did you know the record Salmon caught in the UK was landed by a lady in Scotland?"

"No, I didn't know that."

The girl stepped closer still, and he detected the combination of soap, shampoo and sweat.   It wasn't a particularly pleasant smell, but he singled out the pungent scent from the manufactured aromas, teased it through his nostrils. Using the full motion of her lips, she carefully pronounced, "Ferry-moans."

Ryan frowned. "I've never heard of her," he said.

The girl threw her head back. "Silly," she laughed. "Ferry-moans aren't a person."

He blushed, looked out across the river.

"Ferry-moans come from a person."

"Oh."

"Want me to show you?"

"Well... yeah, I guess so."

"Give me your hand."

He reluctantly placed his lure onto the grass.

"Okay," she said, "these are ferry-moans."

What happened next was like a slap, his senses triggered into overload. She guided his hand down the front of her shorts, rubbed it over the place he'd only seen in friends' magazines. He wanted to pull free, but the movement happened so quickly, so unexpectedly, he stood dumbfounded until she let him go. "Ferry-moans," she said.

He felt sick but excited, embarrassed yet exhilarated, his world tilting as though he'd stepped off the bank and onto a fishing punt. He felt himself go hard and hunched to disguise just exactly how excited he really was.

The girl beamed. "Rub your fingers over your bait. It's why women catch bigger fish. They can sense our ferry-moans."

And just as majestically as she'd appeared, she turned and skipped away, laughing, her hair billowing behind her until the afternoon haze vanished her into thin air.

Ryan never forgot that moment, nor did he see the girl again. He did, however, think about her every night for years, until he'd finally managed to get serious with girls.

He didn't know if it was the Silver Wriggler or these so called 'ferry-moans', but he took two brown trout home for his mother that evening.

***

Ryan placed his rod to one side, never taking his eyes off the girl. His heart thumped beneath his open, sweat-soaked shirt. He guessed he'd stalked around two miles from camp, reassuring the forest guides he wouldn't wander far—it was easy to get carried away, though, especially if you'd spent three miserable days without so much as a nibble, and he wasn't leaving this godforsaken place without something he could mount in a glass case. He'd fished the Earth's seven seas, for Heaven's sake, stalked its big rivers, and all relinquished a specimen for his collection. He'd battled with sharks and barracudas, wrestled with conga eels, giant carp, river perch and pike, and he'd be damned if he wasn't yanking something from the Amazon. A Piranha would be ideal, even a tiddler—it wasn't the first time he'd pictured the crimson-faced predator mounted on his study wall, its dagger teeth impressively exposed.

The girl would see to it. All he needed were 'ferry-moans' and he inched his way closer, expecting the girl to spook and sniff the air like a hare detecting a fox.

The girl was close. He wondered why he was stalking her like the elusive fish in the river. She was a human being, after all, although primitive; her hair was crudely cut—styled, he thought, like one of *The Three Stooges*. She could've been anywhere between twenty and forty, he really couldn't tell because of her emaciated limbs, distended belly and sagging breasts. The red shorts hanging from her hips—obviously a charity token from civilization—in no way tamed her wild disposition. Why not make himself known, then? Talk to her calmly, hold his hands up in submission.

He raised himself, cringing as his knees popped. Making out he hadn't seen her, he looked upstream, inhaling deeply before turning. Their eyes met, the minds behind them worlds apart, but human recognition apparent nonetheless. She looked frightened, ready to bolt. He feigned surprise and bared his palms, offering the universal greeting of a broad smile. Her expression remained one of caution and suspicion, but he was relieved to see her shoulders relax. With his smile firmly in place, he said, "Hello." He jabbed at his chest, announced, "My name is Ryan." This enabled a steady advance and with his hands held out, an idea struck him. He removed his gold divers' watch, making it sparkle prettily in the sun—a Gold Wriggler, he thought, unaware he was panting.

Her expression transformed into something like curiosity, and he was now close enough to make out the rows of pockmarks scarring her cheeks. A red stripe ran under her dark eyes and over the bridge of her pudgy nose. Although he thought this indigenous creature made the red-headed girl look like a lingerie model, and this was by no means a sexual advance, was he really going hard inside his khaki pants? It was the hunt, he mused, the thrill of the hunt.

"Yours," he said, "all yours." Maybe this could be done amicably, he thought. Perhaps he could just hunker down next to her, offer his watch over and...

A shadow crossed her face, and he froze. "Yours," he repeated, trying to disguise the tremor creeping into his voice.

He lifted his smile, unaware he was grinning. That wild instinct was back, he noticed, her irises dancing, the thin muscles in her thighs twitching.

Scared of spooking the girl further, he pulled his hands to his chest and passing a hand over the fingers pinching the watch's strap, masked it and let it fall into his breast pocket. He splayed his fingers as if to say, *Taddahhh!*

Her head cocked and the moment her eyes left his, he lunged, snagging her wrist.

She exploded, bucking and kicking like a snared gazelle. Emitting grunts and pig-like squeals, her struggle abated, long enough for her to turn and strike out, lips peeled back over blackened gums.

Repulsed (he'd never admit to it, but he was also terrified), he swung a panicked haymaker, forcing him into a comedy pirouette. Arms wind-milling, he stumbled back, tottered at the river's edge, and slid down the bank. His boots and clawing fingers stopped him inches from the mud. He didn't see if he'd made contact with the girl, but the fire in his knuckles confirmed a KO blow. He grabbed at the grass, wincing at the needle-jab pain, his ascent clumsy and slow.

Finally, he stood, breathing hard. The girl, as far as he could tell, had fled. "Damn it," he hissed. He ran his fingers through his hair—enough was enough; he'd head back to camp.

And there she was. "Oh no," he panted, "Oh Christ, no."

Partially obscured by an outcrop of reeds, she lay face down in a shallow. The pale balls of her feet bobbed in the lazy currents. Her shorts had slipped, revealing taut buttocks. And her hair, once looking so ridiculous, swayed dreamily in the lapping waves.

He scrambled down the bank, gripped her ankles and hauled her from the wash. As he pulled, her shorts hitched back into place. Mud clung to her, shimmering in the sun. He rolled her over, knowing deep within his racing heart it was too late. Although her mouth gaped and her tongue lolled, the ribcage beneath her flaccid breasts lay dormant. "Shit," he said. He searched the eye that wasn't swollen and split—his doing, he realised—for any signs of life. Clogged by a creamy cataract of river silt, it stared blindly, and he looked away, noticing a section of red tribal paint untouched by mud; it gleamed impossibly bright.

His surroundings now thrummed through mighty speakers, pulsed in time with his heart. A million accusatory eyes studied him from their invisible lairs. The red daubing made him think of poison and he saw himself sprinting through the forest, shadowed assailants close behind. With the camp in sight, he'd think he'd made it, only to swat at a sudden pain stinging the back of his neck. He'd probably have enough time to pluck out the dart, to rationalise it had been traced down the oily spine of a poisonous frog, might even survive its toxins long enough to see one of the girl's tribe leaping from the shadows.

"Calm," he said, "just calm down." The incessant throb joining his heart to his ears abated with every breath, and the threat of imminent danger dissipated. He didn't know how long he'd stared into the water, but the girl's muddy skin had started to crack in the heat.

Pivoting on the spot, he searched the trees, scanned up and downstream. No one had seen him, he thought; he'd be dying a painful death by now if he had. He blinked sweat from his eyes, squinted down at the girl. Apart from the red shorts, she merged with the silt and reeds. In fact, he thought, her legs, now covered in cracked mud, had taken on the appearance of bark.

Camouflage! Yes, he'd push her deeper into the reeds, slop on more mud for good measure. He'd be back at the camp in less than an hour, on a small plane headed back to civilisation in four, sitting in first class on a 747 in under eight. In less than twenty-four hours from this very moment, he'd be sharing a hot bath with a glass of wine. And the girl, he mused, she'd most likely be a stew of chunks sitting in the stomach of a crocodile.

He sank to his knees, gripped the girl's ankles, and shunted her into the reeds. He slathered handfuls of silt over her limbs and torso, looking away as he covered her face. Aware the water would eventually wash the shorts clean—a red flag for her tribe to find—he slipped his hands into the mud and lifted her hips. As he pulled the shorts clear, he balled them up and stuffed them into his pocket.

Invisible, he thought. He could just make out her outline, but supposed that was because he knew she was there.

He grinned, and looking at his glistening fingers, whispered, "Ferry-moans."

***

He'd have to be quick; it was blisteringly hot, and his fingers were already beginning to dry. With the girl—a mere cluster of dead wood—only yards away, he saw the perfect spot. He figured the grassy island fifteen yards out would be teeming with the smaller fish picking at its sunken roots, attracting predators.

Positioned higher up on the bank for a better cast, he pinched the feathers masking the lure's hooks, and transferred the magic bait. He flicked it out just off to the side, let it sink, and began reeling in. Every so often, he twitched the line, imitating a wounded fish.

His first cast produced nothing and he gave the lure a final rub, deciding he'd finally give in to defeat if nothing took.

Again, he placed the bait perfectly. Just something, he thought, anything. If he could just take something away from this hell, he'd—

The line twitched. "That's it," he whispered, slowing the pace, "easy does it."

Without any tentative warning nibbles, the line pulled taut. He struck hard, his rod-tip pulled down, carving a white arc into the water. Off balance, he widened his stance. The line changed direction, heading towards the safety of the bank, towards the reeds... towards the girl. "No you don't," he said, straining.

He'd never fought a fight like it, the surge constant, relentless, no head-shaking, no snapping efforts. Using all his strength and the curve of the rod, he managed to force the monster away from the reeds. The line slashed a V into the water as it passed in front of him. He caught a glimpse of the shape gliding beneath the murk, indiscernible, an indistinct shadow.

The line suddenly fell slack.

He didn't even have time to curse, to complete a single turn of his reel.

The black tendril burst from the water like a torpedo, coiling its way up and around the line. He flicked the rod as though it was an extension of his arm as something revolting had landed on it. The black thing held fast. Incredulous, he watched as it shrunk into itself, hoisting its bloated sack of a body half out of the river. Before he could attempt another shake or abandon the rod altogether, the part still submerged flattened out like a paddle and gave an almighty kick.

For the second time that day, Ryan took a trip over the bank. He slid down on his knees, belly-flopping the water.

Although it was shallow and he broke surface immediately, his boots sank into the silt. He splashed around to face the bank, panic causing him to buck forward before his ankles were swallowed up to his knees. About to make a dash and scramble for the grass, he looked up... and froze.

It was at least seven feet long in its entirety as it hauled itself onto the bank. The black thing had disgorged the hooks, and now rose up onto its bulbous sack, its extending arm reaching high.

"What the hell?" He let his hands and boots sink for fear of attracting attention. If he remained perfectly still, it might...

The black arm flattened out and snapped around towards him. It started weaving back and forth like the hypnotic dance of a cobra.

It's seen me, he thought. No, it's... *smelt* me. There were no discernable features, but he guessed within its oily flesh lay leech-like jaws—razors that would administer a circular saw bite.

The black lump retracted its probing arm.

Ryan eased his hands from the silt. There were only two options available: turn and make for the island, or clamber up the bank and try to out-manoeuvre it. He could try for the opposite bank, but it was at least double the distance, its banks muddy and steep.

The decision was made for him as the blob poured itself down the bank like a barrel of spilt oil.

Managing several clumsy leaps in the shallows, he plunged under, his clothes heavy, his boots blocks of concrete. He kicked hard, awaiting the tug that would take him under for good.

But it never came and his palms found the island's verge with a slap. With fistfuls of root and grass, he hauled himself onto the small outcrop.

Poised and ready to stamp, he scanned the river.

The water was quiet; the thing was nowhere to be seen.

It's waiting, he thought, coiled up beneath me. One false move, just one—

He detected movement on the bank.

From the island it looked like a snake that had just swallowed a bowling ball. It extended and retracted, hauling its distended sack behind it. As it entered the reeds, it weaved and probed with its spade-like head.

The girl, he thought, it's smelt her, prefers its meat dead.

Go, his inner voice urged, go now whilst it's distracted.

The instruction was clear and loud, but the command never reached his limbs. He followed its course as it coiled around and lifted the girl's thigh. Its spade head retracted as though considering its options and, tapering to a point, it lunged, plugging her and thrashing its way in.

Oh god, he thought, it's starting with her insides. Incredulous, he watched as it tunneled its way in, splitting in two, leaving an oily limb to slither up her stomach and between her breasts.

His inner voice screamed: You can make it to the bank! Go! You'll easily—

Again, the black tendril retracted before striking, plugging her mouth, nostrils and ears.

NOW! GO! RIGHT NOW!

The girl lurched onto her side as though she'd been dead for days and writhing with maggots.

He could make it, he decided. The thing was feeding. By the time he'd reached the bank, the thing probably wouldn't have even made it fully out. But what if it did? What if two smaller ones emerged? Quicker ones! And what if there were more?

The girl's right leg twitched.

"Just go," he whispered.

Her leg flexed, kicked, and both feet dragged up to her buttocks. The featureless head slathered with mud pulled free and then slapped back into the slit. Her legs fell open and then pulled back together, and like a marionette plucked from a dusty shelf, she rose up, her arms limp, her chin resting on her chest.

Ryan couldn't feel the warmth spreading across his khakis, nor the throb in his neck; every part of his being tuned in to the figure staggering at the river's edge.

The girl placed a hand to her face, twitched her fingers as though trying them out for the first time. Her head snapped up only to loll back onto her shoulder.

Although he couldn't make out the silt-clogged eye, he could feel its blind stare.

The mud-slicked figure scrunched up her face, her lips pulled back over her teeth. She clawed her fingers and raised them up over her head. Looking as though she were about to either dance or take a dive, she fell to her knees and, sliding effortlessly onto her belly, entered the water like a crocodile.

***

The river continued its lazy stroll into the rain-forest. Ryan stared into the shimmering blanket, not seeing anything but the silver bubbles breaking on the surface as they made their way towards the island.

RAISED BY THE MOON

Ramsey Campbell

It was the scenery that did for him. Having spent the afternoon in avoiding the motorway and enjoying the unhurried country route, Grant reached the foothills only to find the Cavalier refused to climb. He'd driven a mere few hundred yards up the first steep slope when the engine commenced groaning. He should have made time during the week to have it serviced, he thought, feeling like a child caught out by a teacher, except that teaching had shown him what was worse—to be a teacher caught out by a child. He dragged the lever into first gear and ground the accelerator under his heel. The car juddered less than a yard before helplessly backing towards its own smoke.

His surroundings grew derisively irrelevant: the hills quilted with fields, the mountains ridged with pines, the roundish moon trying out its whiteness in the otherwise blue sky. He managed to execute most of a turn as the car slithered backwards and sent it downhill past a Range Rover loaded with a family whose children turned to display their tongues to him. The July heat buttered him as he swung the Cavalier onto a parched verge, where the engine hacked to itself while he glared at the map.

Half the page containing his location was crowded with the fingerprints of mountains. Only the coast was unhampered by their contours. He eased the car off the brown turf and nursed it several digressive miles to the coast road, where a signpost pointed left to Windhill, right to Baiting. Northward had looked as though it might bring him sooner inland to the motorway, and so he took the Baiting route.

He hadn't bargained for the hindrance of the wind. Along the jagged coastline all the trees leaned away from the jumpy sea as though desperate to grasp the land. Before long the barren seaward fields gave way to rocks and stony beaches and there weren't even hedges to fend off the northwester. Whenever the gusts took a breath he smelled how overworked the engine was growing. Beside the road was evidence of the damage the wind could wreak: scattered planks of some construction which, to judge by a ruin a mile farther on, had been a fishmonger's stall. Then the doggedly spiky hedge to his right winced inland, revealing an arc of cottages as white as the moon would be when the sky went out. Perhaps someone in the village could repair the car or Grant would find a room for the night—preferably both.

The ends of the half-mile arc of cottages were joined across the inlet by a submerged wall or a path that divided the prancing sea from the less restless bay. The far end was marked by a lone block of colour, a red telephone box planted in the water by a trick of perspective. His glimpse of a glistening object crouched or heaped in front of it had to be another misperception; when he returned his attention to the view once he'd finished tussling with the wheel as a gust tried to shove the car across the road, he saw no sign of life.

The car was panting and shivering by the time he reached the first cottage. A vicious wind that smelled of fish stung his skin as he eased his rusty door shut and peered tearfully at the buildings opposite. He thought all the windows were curtained with net until he realised the whiteness was salt, which had also scoured the front doors pale. In the very first window a handwritten sign offered ROOM. The wind hustled him across the road, which was strewn with various conditions of seaweed, to the fish-faced knocker on a door that had once been black.

More of the salt that gritted under his fingers was lodged in the hinge. He had to dig his thumb into the gaping mouth to heave the fish-head high and slam it against the metal plate. He heard the blow fall flat in not much of a passage and a woman's voice demanding shrilly "Who wants us now?"

The nearest to a response was an irregular series of slow footsteps that ended behind the door, which was dragged wide by a man who filled most of the opening. Grant couldn't tell how much of his volume he owed to his cable-knit jersey and loose trousers, but the bulk of his face drooped like perished rubber from his cheekbones. Salt might account for the redness of his small eyes, though perhaps anxiety had turned his sparse hair and dense eyebrows white. He hugged himself and shivered and glanced past his visitor, presumably at the wind. Parting his thick lips with a tongue as ashen, he mumbled "Where have you come from?"

"Liverpool."

"Don't know it," the man said, and seemed ready to use that as an excuse to close the door.

A woman plodded out of the kitchen at the end of the cramped dingy hall. She looked as though marriage had transformed her into a version of the man, shorter but broader to compensate and with hair at least as white, not to mention clothes uncomfortably similar to his. "Bring him in," she urged.

"What are you looking for?" her husband muttered.

"Someone who can fix my car and a room if I'll need one."

"Twenty miles up the coast."

"I don't think it'll last that far. Won't they come here?"

"Of course they will if they're wanted, Tom. Let him in."

"You're staying, then."

"I expect I may have to. Can I phone first?"

"If you've the money you can give it a tackle."

"How much will it take?" When Tom's sole answer was a stare, Grant tried "How much do you want?"

"Me, nothing. Nor her either. Phone's up the road."

Grant was turning away, not without relief, when the woman said "Won't he need the number? Tommy and his Fiona."

"I know that. Did you get it?" Tom challenged Grant.

"I don't think—"

"Better start, then. Five. Three. Three. Five," Tom said and shut the door.

Grant gave in to an incredulous laugh that politeness required him to muffle. Perhaps another cottage might be more welcoming, he thought with dwindling conviction as he progressed along the seafront. He could hardly see through any of the windows, and such furniture as he could distinguish, by no means in every room, looked encrusted with more than dimness. The few shops might have belonged to fishmongers; one window displayed a dusty plastic lobster on a marble slab also bearing stains suggestive of the prints of large wet hands. The last shop must have been more general, given the debris scattered about the bare floor—distorted but unopened tins, a disordered newspaper whose single legible headline said **FISH STOCKS DROP**, and was there a dead cat in the darkest corner? Beyond two farther cottages was the refuge of the phone box.

Perhaps refuge was too strong a word. Slime on the floor must indicate that it hadn't been out of reach of the last high tide. A fishy smell that had accompanied him along the seafront was also present, presumably borne by the wind that kept lancing the trapped heat with chill. Vandalism appeared to have invaded even this little community; the phone directory was strewn across the metal shelf below the coin-box in fragments so sodden they looked chewed. Grant had to adjust the rakish handset on its hook to obtain a tone before he dragged the indisposed dial to the numbers he'd repeated all the way to the box. He was trying to distinguish whether he was hearing static or simply the waves when a man's brusque practically Scottish voice said "Beach."

"You aren't a garage, then."

"Who says I'm not? Beach's Garage."

"I'm with you now," Grant said, though feeling much as he had when Tom translated his wife's mnemonic. "And you fix cars."

"I'd be on the scrapheap if I didn't."

"Good," Grant blurted and to compensate "I mean, I've got one for you."

"Lucky me."

"It's a Cavalier that wouldn't go uphill."

"Can't say a word about it 'til I've seen it. All I want to know is where you are."

"Twenty miles south of you, they tell me."

"I don't need to ask who." After a pause during which Grant felt sought by the chill and the piscine smell, the repairman said "I can't be there before dark."

"You think I should take a room."

"I don't tell anybody what to do. Invited you in as well, did they?"

The man's thriftiness with language was affecting Grant much as unresponsive pupils did. "Shouldn't they have?" he retorted.

"They'll do their best for you, Tom and Fiona. They need the cash."

"How did you know who they were?"

"There's always some that won't be driven out of their homes. A couple, anyway."

"Driven."

When competing at brevity brought no answer, Grant was about to add to his words when the man said, "You won't see many fish round Baiting anymore."

Grant heard the basis of a geography lesson in this. "So they've had to adapt to living off tourists."

"And travellers and whatever else they catch." The repairman interrupted himself with a cough that might have been a mirthless laugh. "Anyway, that's their business. I'll be there first thing in the morning."

The phone commenced droning like a fly attracted by the fishy smell until Grant stubbed his thumb on the hook. He dug the crumpled number of the holiday cottage out of his jeans and dialled, rousing only a bell that repeated itself as insistently as the waves for surely longer than his fellow students could have disagreed over who should answer it, even if they sustained the argument with a drink and quite possibly a toke to boot. No doubt they were expecting him to arrive ahead of them and set about organising as usual. He dropped the receiver onto its prongs and forced open the arthritic door.

He might have returned to his car along the sea wall, the top of which was nearly two feet wide, if waves hadn't been spilling over much of its length. There appeared to be little else to describe to any class he would teach; rubble was piled so high in the occasional alleys between the cottages that he couldn't even see behind them. The bay within the wall swarmed with infant waves, obscuring his view of whatever he kept glimpsing beneath them: probably the tops of pillars reinforcing the wall, except that the objects were irregularly spaced—the tips of a natural rock formation the wall had followed, then, although the string of blurred shapes put him in mind of a series of reflections of the moon. He was no closer to identifying them by the time he reached the Cavalier.

He manhandled his suitcase through the gap the creaky boot vouchsafed him and tramped across the road. He was hesitating over reaching for the knocker when the cottage door sprang open. He was bracing himself to be confronted by the husband, which must be why the sight of the woman's upturned face was disconcerting. "Get in, then," she exhorted with what could have been intended as rough humour.

Perhaps she was eager to shut out the wind that was trying all the inner doors, unless she wanted to exclude the smell. More of that lingered once Grant slammed the door than he found inviting. "Let's have you up," the woman said.

She'd hardly set one shabbily slippered foot on the lowest of the narrow uncarpeted stairs that bisected the hall when she swung round to eye him. "First time away?"

"Nothing like."

"Just your case looks so new."

"My parents bought me a set of them when I started college."

"We never had any children. What's your name, anyway?" she added with a fierceness he hoped she was directing at herself. "You know ours."

"Bill Grant."

"Good and strong," she said, giving him a slow appreciative blink before stumping shapelessly upwards to thump the first door open with her buttocks. The rumpled sea widened beyond the small window as he followed her into the room. He'd passed a number of framed photographs on his way upstairs, and here above the sink was yet another grey image of a man, nondescript except for the fish he was measuring between his hands. As in the other pictures, he was her husband Tom. His presence helped the furniture—a barely even single bed, a barren dressing-table, a wardrobe no larger than a phone box—make the room feel yet more confined. "Anything like home?" Fiona said.

It did remind him somewhat of his bedroom when he was half his size. "Something," he admitted.

"You want to feel at home if you go anywhere. I know I would." Having stared at him as though to ensure some of her meaning remained, she reached up to grab his shoulders with her cold swollen hands as an aid to squeezing past him. "We'll call you when it's time to put our snouts in the trough," she said.

He listened to the series of receding creaks her descent extracted from the stairs, and then he relieved his suitcase of the items he would need for an overnight stay, feeling absurdly as if he were preparing for a swift escape. Once he'd ventured across the tiny strident landing to the bathroom, a tiled white cell occupied by three dripping sweaters pegged on a rope above the bath and by a chilly damp that clung to him, he sat next to his pyjamas on the bed to scribble notes for a geography lesson based on Baiting, then sidled between the sink and the foot of the bed to the window.

It seemed his powers of observation needed work. The whitish rounded underwater blobs were closer together and to the middle of the sea wall than he remembered, unless any of them had indeed been a version of the moon, which was presently invisible above the roof. Perhaps he would soon be able to identify them, since the waves were progressing towards relative calm. He left his bulky bunch of keys on the windowsill before lying down to listen to the insistent susurration, which was occasionally interrupted by a plop that led him to believe the sea was less uninhabited than the repairman had said. He grew tired of craning to catch sight of whatever kept leaving ripples inside the sea wall, and by the time Fiona called "Ready" up the stairs, an invitation reminiscent of the beginning of a game, he was shelving towards sleep.

He must have been near to dreaming while awake, since he imagined that a face had edged out of hiding to watch him sit up. It might have been dour Tom's in the photograph or the moon that had crept into view above the bay, possibly appending at least one blob to the cluster along the sea wall. "I'll be down," Grant shouted loud enough, he hoped, to finish wakening himself.

He wasn't expecting to eat in the kitchen, on a table whose unfolding scarcely left room for three hard straight chairs and a stained black range crowned with bubbling saucepans and, beneath a small window that grudgingly twilighted the room, a massive stone sink. He'd thought a fishy smell that had kept him company upstairs was carried by the wind, but now he realised it might also have been seeping up from the kitchen. He was exerting himself to look entertained when Tom frowned across the table at him. "She ought to have asked you to pay in advance."

"Oh, Tom, he's nothing but a youngster."

Grant was a little too much of one to appreciate being described that way. "Can I give you a cheque and a card?"

"And your name and address."

"Let's have you sitting down first," Fiona cried, stirring a pan that aggravated the smell.

Grant fumbled in the pocket of his jeans for the cheque book and card wallet. "How much am I going to owe you?"

Tom glowered at his soup-bowl as though ashamed to ask. "Thirty if you're here for breakfast."

"Of course he will be, Tom."

"If he isn't sick of it by then."

Grant wrote a cheque in his best blackboard handwriting and slid it with his guarantee card and driving licence across the table. "Grant's the word, eh?" Tom grumbled, poking at the cards with a thick flabby forefinger whose nail was bitten raw. "She said you were a student, right enough."

"I teach as well," Grant was provoked into retorting. "That'll be my life."

"So what are you planning to fill their dim little heads with?"

"I wouldn't mind telling them the story of your village."

"Few years since it's been that." Tom finished scrutinising the cheque and folded it twice to slip into his trousers pocket, then stared at or through his guest. "On a night like this there'd be so many fish we'd have to bring the nets in before dawn or have them snapped."

"Nights like this make me want to swim," Fiona said, and perhaps more relevantly, "He used to like taking the boat out then."

She ladled soup into three decidedly various bowls and watched with Tom while Grant committed his stained spoon to the viscous milky liquid. It explained the smell in the kitchen and tasted just not too strongly of it to be palatable. "There are still fish, then," he said, and when his hosts met this with identical small-eyed stares, "Good. Good."

"We've given up the fishing. We've come to an arrangement," said Tom.

Grant sensed that was as much as he would say about it, presumably resenting the loss of his independence. Nobody spoke until the bowls were empty, nor indeed until Fiona had served three platefuls of flaccid whitish meat accompanied by heaps of mush, apparently potatoes and some previously green vegetable. More of the meat finished gently quivering to itself in an indistinguishable lump on a platter. Grant thought rather than hoped it might be tripe, but unless the taste of the soup had lodged in his mouth, the main course wasn't mammalian. Having been watched throughout two rubbery mouthfuls, he felt expected to say at least, "That's good too. What is it?"

"All there is to eat round here," Tom said in a sudden dull rage.

"Now, Tom, it's not his fault."

"It's people's like his." Tom scowled at his dinner and then at the guest. "Want to know what you want to tell the sprats you're supposed to be teaching?"

"I believe I do, but if you'd like—"

"About time they were told to stop using cars for a start. And if the poor deprived mites can't live without them, tell them not to take them places they don't need to go."

"Saints, Tom, they're only youngsters."

"They'll grow up, won't they, if the world doesn't conk out first." With renewed ire he said to Grant, "They need to do without their fridges and their freezers and their microwaves and whatever else is upsetting things."

Grant felt both accused of too much urban living and uneasy about how the meat was stored. Since no refrigerator was visible, he hoped it was fresh. He fed himself mouthfuls to be done with it and dinner generally, but hadn't completed the labour when he swallowed in order to speak. "At least you aren't alone, then."

"It's in your cities people go off and leave each other," muttered Tom.

"No, I mean you aren't the only ones in your village. I got the idea from your friend Mr. Beach you were."

Tom looked ready to deny any friendship, but it seemed he was preparing to demand, "Calling him a liar, are you?"

"I wouldn't say a liar, just mistaken," Grant said, nodding at the wall the cottage shared with its neighbour. His hosts merely eyed him as though they couldn't hear the renewed sounds beyond the wall, a floundering and shuffling that brought to mind someone old or otherwise incapacitated. "Rats?" he was compelled to assume.

"We've seen a few of those in our time," said Tom, continuing to regard him.

If that was meant for wit, Grant found it offered no more than the least of the children he'd had to teach. Some acoustic effect made the rat sound much larger as it scuffed along the far side of the wall before receding into the other cottage. Rather than risk stirring it or his hosts up further, Grant concentrated on downing enough of his meal to allow him to push away his plate and mime fullness. He was certainly full of a taste not altogether reminiscent of fish; he felt as though he were trying to swim through it, or it through him. When he drank a glass of the pitcher of water that had been the solitary accompaniment to the meal, he thought the taste was in there too.

Fiona cleared the plates into the sink, and that was the end of dinner. "Shall I help?" Grant had been brought up to offer.

"That's her work."

Since Fiona smiled indulgently at that, Grant didn't feel entitled to disagree. "I'd better go and phone, then."

He imagined he saw a pale shape lurch away from the window into the unspecific dimness—it must have been Fiona's reflection as she turned to blink at him. "He said you had."

"I ought to let my friends know I won't be seeing them tonight."

"They'll know when you don't, won't they? We don't want the waves carrying you off." Wiping her hands on a cloth that might have been part of someone's discarded garment, she pulled out a drawer beside the sink. "Stay in and we'll play a few games."

While the battered cardboard box she opened on the table was labelled Ludo, that wasn't quite what it contained. Rattling about on top of the familiar board inside the box were several fragments of a substance Grant told himself wasn't bone. "We make our own amusement round here," Fiona said. "We use whatever's sent us."

"He's not your lad."

"He could be."

The scrape of Grant's chair on the stone floor went some way towards expressing his discomfort. "I'll phone now," he said.

"Not driving, are you?" Tom enquired.

"Not at all." Grant couldn't be bothered resenting whatever the question implied. "I'm going to enjoy the walk."

"He'll be back soon for you to play with," Tom told his wife.

She turned to gaze out at the dark while Tom's stare weighed on their visitor, who stood up. "I won't need a key, will I?"

"We'll be waiting for you," Fiona mumbled.

Grant sensed tension as oppressive as a storm, and didn't thank the bare floorboards for amplifying his retreat along the hall. He seized the clammy latch and hauled the front door open. The night was almost stagnant. Subdued waves smoothed themselves out on the black water beyond the sea wall, inside which the bay chattered silently with whiteness beneath the incomplete mask of a moon a few days short of full. An odour he no longer thought it adequate to call fishy lingered in the humid air or inside him as he hurried towards the phone box.

The heat left over from the day more than kept pace with him. The infrequent jab of chill wind simply encouraged the smell. He wondered if an allergy to whatever he'd eaten was beginning to make itself felt in a recurrent sensation, expanding through him from his stomach, that his flesh was turning rubbery. The cottages had grown intensely present as chunks of moon fallen to earth, and seemed less deserted than he'd taken them to be: the moonlight showed that patches of some of the windows had been rubbed or breathed or even licked imperfectly clear. Once he thought faces rose like flotsam to watch him from the depths of three successive cottages, unless the same face was following him from house to ruined house. When he failed to restrain himself from looking, of course there was only moonlit dimness, and no dead cat in the general store. He did his best to scoff at himself as he reached the phone box.

Inside, the smell was lying in wait for him. He held the door open with his foot, though that admitted not only the infrequent wind but also more of the light that made his hand appear as pale as the receiver in it was black. His clumsy swollen fingers found the number in his pocket and held the scrap of paper against the inside of a frame that had once contained a mirror above the phone. Having managed to dial, he returned the paper to its niche against his unreasonably flabby thigh and clutched the receiver to his face with both hands. The fourth twosome of rings was parted by a clatter that let sounds of revelry at him, and belatedly a voice. "Who's this?"

For longer than a breath Grant felt as if he was being forced to stand up in class for a question he couldn't answer, and had to turn it back on the questioner. "It's Ian, isn't it?"

"Bill," Ian said, and shouted it to their friends. "Where have you got to?" he eventually thought to ask.

"I've broken down on the coast. I'm getting the car fixed tomorrow."

"When are we seeing you?"

"I told you, tomorrow," Grant said, though the notion felt remote in more ways than he could name.

"Have a drink for us, then, and we will for you. Won't we, you crew?"

The enthusiasm this aroused fell short of Grant, not least because he'd been reminded of the water accompanying dinner, a memory that revived the taste of the meal. "Don't get too pissed to drive tomorrow," Ian advised and made way for a chorus of drunken encouragement followed by the hungry buzz of the receiver.

Grant planted the receiver on its hook and shoved himself out of the box. Even if Baiting had boasted a pub, he would have made straight for his room; just now, supine was the only position that appealed to him. As the phone box shut with a muted thud that emphasised the desertion of the seafront, he set out along the top of the submerged wall.

It was broad enough for him to feel safe even if he wobbled—luckily for his career, however distant that seemed, teachers didn't have to be able to swim. He wouldn't have minded being able to progress at more than a shuffle towards the landmark of his car blackened by the moonlight, but the unsynchronised restlessness flanking him made him feel less than stable, as if he was advancing through some unfamiliar medium. The luminous reflection of the arc of cottages hung beneath them, a lower jaw whose unrest suggested it was eager to become a knowing grin. The shape of the bay must be causing ripples to resemble large slow bubbles above the huddle of round whitish shapes along the middle of the sea wall. He still couldn't make them out, nor how many images of the moon were tracking him on or just beneath the surface of the inlet. The closer he came to the halfway mark, the larger the bubbles appeared to grow. He was within a few yards of them and feeling mesmerised by his own pace and by the whispers of the sea, when he heard a protracted stealthy wallowing behind him. He turned to find he had company on the far end of the wall.

It must be a swimmer, he told himself. Its glistening suggested it was wearing a wet suit rendered pallid by the moon; surely it couldn't be naked. Was the crouched figure making a joke of his progress? As it began to drag its feet, which struck him as unnecessarily large, along the wall, it looked no more at home on the path than he felt. Its head was bent low, and yet he had the disconcerting impression that it was presenting its face to him. It had shuffled several paces before he was able to grasp that he would rather outdistance it than see it in greater detail. He swung around and faltered just one step in the direction of his car. While his attention had been snared, another figure as squat and pale and dripping had set out for him from the opposite end of the wall.

He was paralysed by the spectacle of the pair converging effortfully but inexorably on him, the faces on their lowered heads indisputably towards him, until a movement let him peer in desperation at the farthest cottage. The front door had opened, and over the car roof he saw Tom. "Can you come and help me?" Grant shouted, stumbling towards him along the wall.

The cottages flattened and shrank his voice and sent him Tom's across the bay. "No need for that."

"There is," Grant pleaded. "That's in my way."

"Rude bugger."

Grant had to struggle to understand this meant him. It added itself to the sight of the advancing figure pallid as the underside of a dead fish. The closer it shuffled, the less it appeared to have for a face. "What are they?" he cried.

"They're all the moon brings us these days," Tom said, audibly holding Grant or people like him responsible, and stepped out of the cottage. He was naked, like the figures on the wall. The revelation arrested Grant while Tom plodded to the car. Indeed, he watched Tom unlock it and climb in before this sent him forward. "Stop that," he yelled. "What do you think you're doing? Get out of my car."

The Cavalier was no more likely to start first time for a naked driver than it ever did for him, he promised himself. Then it spluttered out a mass of fumes and performed a screeching U-turn. "Come back," Grant screamed. "You can't do that. You're polluting your environment."

No doubt his protests went unheard over the roaring of the engine. The sound took its time over dwindling once the coastline hid the car. The squat whitish shapes had halted once Grant had begun shouting. He strode at the figure crouched between him and the cottage and, since it didn't retreat, with as little effect at the other. He was repeating the manoeuvre, feeling like a puppet of his mounting panic, when that was aggravated by a burst of mirth. Fiona had appeared in the cottage doorway and was laughing at him. "Just jump in," she called across the water.

He didn't care how childish his answer sounded if she was capable of saving him. "I can't swim."

"What, a big strong lad like you?" Her heartiness increased as she declared "You can now. You can float, at any rate. Give it a try. We'll have to feed you up."

Beyond the spur of the coastline the sound of the car rose to a harsh note that was terminated by a massive splash. "That's the end of that," Fiona called. "You can be one of my big babies instead."

Grant's mind was refusing to encompass the implications of this when Tom came weltering like a half-submerged lump of the moon around the bay. Grant dashed along the sea wall, away from Fiona and Tom. He was almost at the middle section when he saw far too much in the water: not just the way that section could be opened as a gate, but the pallid roundish upturned faces that were clustered alongside. They must be holding their breath to have grown clear at last, their small flat unblinking eyes and, beneath the noseless nostrils, perfectly round mouths gaping in hunger that looked like surprise. As he wavered, terrified to pass above them, he had a final insight that he could have passed on to a classroom of pupils: the creatures must be waiting to open the gate and let in the tide and any fish it carried. "Don't mind them," Fiona shouted. "They don't mind we eat their dead. They even bring them now."

An upsurge of the fishy taste worse than nausea made Grant stagger along the wall. The waiting shape crouched forward, displaying the round-mouthed emotionless face altogether too high on its plump skull. Hands as whitish and as fat jerked up from the bay, snatching at Grant's feet. "That's the way, show him he's one of us," Fiona urged, casting off her clothes as she hurried to the water's edge.

She must have been encouraging Grant's tormentors to introduce him to the water. In a moment fingers caught his ankles and overbalanced him. His frantic instinctive response was to hurl himself away from them, into the open sea. Drowning seemed the most attractive prospect left to him.

The taste expanded through him, ousting the chill of the water with a sensation he was afraid to name. When he realised it was the experience of floating, he let out a howl that merely cleared his mouth of water. Too many pallid shapes for him to count were heaving themselves over the wall to surround him. He flailed his limbs and then tried holding them still, desperate to find a way of making himself sink. There was none. "Don't worry," Fiona shouted as she sloshed across the bay towards him, "you'll soon get used to our new member of the family," and, in what felt like the last of his sanity, Grant wondered if she was addressing his captors or Tom.

A SUMMER ON QUIET ISLAND

Cody Goodfellow

From the porch glider on the verandah of the Myrick house, Joe watched the island kids play baseball. Fog thick as cotton wadding rolled overhead, and reached feathery fingers among the trees that defined the dusty field. The scene felt like a silent movie, leeched of all color but sepia and white, the kids hopping and skipping nervously as if captured by a hand-cranked camera—and of course, none of them made a sound.

The foghorn's low groan rolled over the island like a broken bell in a church somewhere up above the fog, shaking the brittle, warped bay window behind him, but nobody else seemed to notice. All of them but Joe had been born here, and were probably used to it by now. And most of them were deaf from birth, so they must like it loud enough to make their china dance.

Mom taught him it was wrong to stare, but what else could you do? Watching the island kids play wasn't even funny anymore. At home, when a kid had a clubfoot or a raspberry birthmark, you could get a good laugh off him. But here, there was something wrong with everyone. They walked like they had glass in their pants. They stared into space sometimes, like they were sleeping on their feet. And sometimes, they pointed at him on the porch and their mouths opened and a husky, glottal croak came out, like a deaf mute's idea of laughter.

Quiet Island took some getting used to.

Aunt Meg whisked out onto the porch and set a mug of hot cocoa beside him. She ruffled his hair and clucked contentedly, as if she didn't notice how he flinched. He liked Aunt Meg, but even now, it was hard to look at her. He knew the red sores and turbid papules that made a runny ruin of her smile and ran riot over her hands weren't contagious. But he couldn't abide the feel of that hand, coarse from housework and ribboned by weird raised scars with cat's-claw-shaped growths erupting out of them, the inflamed impression of hunger they conveyed, as if they might leap like fire from her skin to his. But she was family; the Myricks were all the family he had.

When Joe's Mom went back into rehab, they sent him to stay with his father's sister's family on Quiet Island. He didn't know who tracked them down or made the arrangements. He'd never met anyone from his father's family. His mother told Joe that his father came from an island and was a fisherman, but he had to leave. He went up to Alaska to work the canneries and was gone for whole seasons of Joe's life. When Joe was seven, his father didn't come back from Alaska and Mom didn't look for him to return. Joe was thirteen and he wanted to believe this was only temporary.

Quiet Island is a mile long and less than a quarter mile wide at the south end, where a shallow bay shelters the pier and the meager fleet of fishing boats. In the constant fog, the uneven, restless terrain seems to shrink down to the rock immediately underfoot. The fog hides the land and carries the sound of the ocean to one's ear, so every step seems like land's end.

A sliver of castaway land thirty miles off the coast, Quiet Island was settled by a loose confederation of pilgrims who forsook the mainland over some long-forgotten grievance. Thaddeus Fleming, the de facto leader of the settlers, cut off all ties with the outside world and embarked on a muted but thorough campaign to erase Quiet Island from all maps at the time. Somehow, the oversight persisted until the U.S. Geological Survey stumbled upon them with their satellites.

There were thirty houses on the island, including the old Fleming house, which served as the island's town hall after the last of the Fleming men was lost at sea. Fourteen houses were occupied. The clans that survived tended to huddle together and many of the occupied houses—the ones with lantern lights in the windows and some remnant of paint on the exterior walls—had expanded upwards and outwards with varying degrees of forethought and execution. A half-timber and brick addition on one side of the Myrick house stood tall and true enough to put its clapboard neighbors to shame, while the wing on the other side lacked the insulation of a chicken coop and listed audibly in the wind.

Joe was there nearly a week before he realized he had seen no animals. No dogs, no cats, no cows, pigs or chickens, though he saw the overgrown remains of corrals and collapsed barns everywhere.

He stopped once to explore the burned out ruin of a house. The foundation was bearded in berry bushes and weeds, but the stones were still black in their cracks and crevices. Joe climbed the front steps to nowhere and looked down into the surprisingly deep hollow of the cellar. If it was of a piece with the boxy two-story houses everyone else lived in, the house must have been like a tree, as big beneath the ground as above it.

An old man on a bicycle stopped on the road and glared. He stood straddling the rusty green beach cruiser pointed at Joe, or at the ruin, then howled a long, drawn-out sound like "Nyeeeyeeooofadoowuh." His other hand, clutched at his throat to feel the ear-splitting scream, had only two fingers on it, and was mottled with horrid scars.

Joe jumped off the steps and backed away from the cyclist. One of his ears was melted off and the twitching, awkward posture of his raincoated form when he mounted the pedals and sped away spoke of even worse disfigurement underneath.

When Joe got back, he wrote a note to Grandma Amelia and slid it to her. She looked at it and folded it, went on chopping onions for soup. His cousin Lorna flounced through the room a minute later and glanced at the note. "The Rowbottom house burned down. People said your father did it."

"That's a lie!" It was weird, how nobody here would ever tell him to keep his voice down. Uncle Tab was deaf, Meg was deaf and mute, and he could never tell about Grandma.

"That's why he had to leave."

Joe could think of a thousand good reasons why someone would want to leave here, but he held his tongue. Nobody ever talked to him about his father.

"He wanted to marry Winnie Rowbottom, but her father said he wasn't good enough. He left, and when he came back—ow!"

Grandma Amelia made a "sorry" gesture and wiped Lorna's blood off her knife with a dishrag.

It wasn't so bad here, really, except for meals, which were the same every day. Steelcut oatmeal for breakfast, tuna sandwiches for lunch and every night, the chowder.

A pot of it was always simmering on the stove, making the house smell like a dirty aquarium. Chowder, they called it, but it wasn't like any chowder he'd ever heard of. It was red and thick and loaded with herbs and onions to hide the oily, rancid stock loaded with rubbery, spherical beads that popped between his teeth. It tasted like blood, but nobody else at the table seemed to mind.

Joe often thought that if only someone knocked over the big black cauldron, they would have to eat something else, but he knew there was nothing but canned tuna and oatmeal in the pantry, nothing in the fridge but tubs of cold chowder stock. The store shelves at the market were mostly empty and everyone paid with food stamps for what little there was. The pretty redheaded girl who ran the store in the afternoons never paid attention, but there was no candy to steal. Domino's didn't deliver to Quiet Island.

Once, he asked if it was fish eggs and blood. Nobody answered, but Aunt Meg cried and left the table. Uncle Tab sent him to bed hungry. He didn't ask about the chowder after that.

Grandma Amelia's hands shook worse than usual as she ladled out the chowder tonight. Her fingers jumped and crabbed up with a will of their own. Her tongue jutted out of her mouth and she dropped the ladle into Joe's bowl.

Splattered with chowder, Joe jumped back from his chair and shouted, "What the fuck," but nobody was watching him.

Grandma's hands jerked and shredded an invisible bag that seemed to fall over her face. Aunt Meg held her down and pulled her tongue out of her throat. Lorna picked up the ladle and resumed serving the chowder.

He could walk the length of the island in less than ten minutes, from the harbor and the general store at the south end to the lighthouse on the rocks at the northern tip, but the broken land offered hollows and meandering canyons, where the ruins of generations of tree houses and forts had collapsed or been engulfed by the pickleweed and blood-red ice plant. He would sneak into them to puff a smoke or a bowl from his tiny stash of weed, and goof on the graffiti kids had etched into the wood with charcoal. It seemed like every generation of kids had evolved their own written language from scratch; some were pictographs a Neanderthal would have sneered at, while others had more symbols than Chinese, and were as complex as they were indecipherable. A few words or names were in plain English, but hardly legible.

Miss Bly, the mule-faced spinster who kept the school in the Smoody house's parlor, would have caned them for their atrocious penmanship, to say nothing of the vaguely obscene images of naïve yet inventive acts of sexual congress. The boys were absurdly well-endowed stick and balloon figures, but their partners were fancifully and fully rendered, with voluptuous details and lovingly rendered expressions that only made it more obscene, since they were all fish.

Other days, he went down to the tidepools, but there wasn't much to see. The waves gushed over the black basalt and flushed out the seemingly bottomless pits in the rocky bluffs at the foot of the cliffs all around the island. The flitting white shapes in the pools were condoms and bits of bleached plastic shopping bags, and the colorful jewels on the walls were bits of glass. At low tide, the still water in the pools glittered with a rainbow gasoline sheen that was prettier than any fish, anyway.

It was depressing, but it beat looking out at the ocean. The rolling waves were like moving walls between Joe and everything good in the world. Uncle Tab told him the island was a lone peak on an abyssal plain almost two miles deep, but when he looked out at the sea, it was like a hateful huge living thing, shoving the island farther away from the mainland every day.

The modest armada of boats drifted at anchor in the still black waters in the crook of the harbor and the men sat or kicked the ground in front of the harbormaster's shack from before dawn to breakfast and the harbormaster's horn, breaking up in surly groups to work on other projects or skulk in someone's barnyard to drink. It was not yet the season, Aunt Meg said when he asked why nobody went out to sea.

The fishing had dwindled to nothing long before anyone on the island was born, except for the quilting circle and old Ichabod Smoody, the harbormaster. The waters around Quiet Island were dead for fifty miles and outside that they couldn't compete with the big commercial boats, with their sonar tracking and their nets. They used the old ways and trusted in the sea and the sea still kept its promise to the first settlers. It gave them what they needed and more than most folks on the mainland could expect, but one had to be patient.

Not that Joe gave two shits for fishing, but all the kids his age, boys and girls worked the boats and huddled in their own clique at the edge of the fishermen. When the dark began to dissolve into cold green fire on the eastern horizon, the fishermen gathered and waited as Ichabod settled into his rowboat with a box across his lap and was rowed out beyond the breakwater by his sullen great grandson, a hulking, hunchbacked brute with a harelip that split his nose like a bat's snout.

Joe hung out just within earshot of the other teenagers. Lorna seemed to be the hub of the group, but she never introduced him around. The other kids clearly asked about him in whispers or signs, but she shrugged as if she didn't know him, he wasn't worth knowing, or he didn't really exist.

When Ichabod returned, he hobbled up the pier to the porch of his shack before he ceremoniously signed that the tide was wrong and the catch was not coming. The fishermen expelled a collective grunt and dispersed. The kids idled and smoked a while before breaking up. One day, Joe said, "fuck it," and went over.

He tucked the earbuds of his iPod into his breast pocket and edged closer with a wistful smile on his face. "Hi, I'm—"

A big redheaded boy with a pug's face wheeled on him and socked him in the eye without any warning, without saying a word, and turned back to finish telling a joke with his hands.

Joe got up and tried to muster the rage to call him out, but there was no opening in the group and he didn't feel anger. He just felt shock and fear and a dull ache as his eye closed over and he felt nine years old.

Aunt Meg wrote him he should stay away from the fishermen, especially after they'd gotten bad news. "When their blood is up, they need someone to punch. If you hadn't come along, they would have started up with each other, sure enough."

When she came home for supper, Lorna smirked at him as she hurried upstairs to wash up. "Sorry about your eye, cousin. My mates thought you were queer."

Did she mean gay? He could never tell for sure with the way they talked... the few of them who could or did. He followed her up the stairs and down the hall, past all those doors with dust piling up against the thresholds. "Nobody gave me a chance. I was just trying to talk to them. And I'm not... I'm straight."

"They won't ever believe that now."

"What did I do? I didn't hit on him, I was just trying to—"

"You didn't fight him." She closed the door in his face.

Dinner was late.

Grandma Amelia didn't come down from her room. Aunt Meg loomed over the stove. Uncle Tab sat at the dinner table with a bunch of nautical maps and notes spread everywhere. The smell of the chowder on the stove turned Joe's stomach with renewed vigor, as if the stock had begun to turn.

They did things differently here, that was all. It was just temporary. They did the best they could, doing what they had to do to survive out here and if they were meant to live somewhere else, why, they would have been born there.

They were the only family he had left, the only ones who would take him in.

The aroma of the chowder on the stove grew more briny and bitter, and shortly the kitchen filled with smoke. Aunt Meg had dozed off on her feet in front of the stove, but they served it anyway. The burst eggs in the black soup tasted like licking a weak, leaking battery.

"Soup's off," Uncle Tab muttered, but he dutifully slurped the last scorched dregs from his chipped china bowl. "But soon the catch'll be in. Tomorrow, if the tides are right. Boy here ought to learn to work."

"How much does it pay?" Joe said in a deep voice.

"I'll take it out of your room and board," Tab chuckled.

Aunt Meg signed something too fast for Joe to catch anything, but it included several emphatic No's.

"If the boy's going to stay here, he'll have to make himself useful. He starts tomorrow." Rapping his arthritic fist on the table like a gavel, Tab rose and left the room.

Joe jumped as he felt something brush against his leg, teasingly like a cat. Lorna smirked at him as she got up to clear the dishes.

He went out on the porch after dinner, and he chanced to see the women of the island going to work. A line of twelve of them, all pregnant, stooped over gravid bellies, some hobbling along with canes. Most of them were not much older than Lorna, but some were Aunt Meg's age. He watched them pass out of sight before he followed them, lighting a cigarette and popping in his earbuds.

They went into the little warehouse at the edge of the harbor. He'd heard Lorna call it the hatchery, but he figured it was abandoned like most of the buildings on the island. The big barn doors were chained, and the windows were boarded up, but a deadfall of discarded crab cages piled against the leeward wall nearly reached the roof and he managed to climb it and perch uneasily before a slot between white, warped shingles and peek inside.

Beneath him, a young girl lay on a cot with her legs in stirrups, just like at the doctor's office. Joe recognized her from the store. She was a few years older than him and watched the counter for her father.

The doctor was there and an old woman with glazed eggs for eyes, stroking the pretty girl's lovely burnished red hair. She wasn't pregnant, that Joe could see, and hadn't been with the others.

The cot was enclosed in black rubber curtains and a big rubber pouch hung on a hook over the doctor's head. A hose from it trailed on the floor and the doctor stuck it under the girl's skirt.

Joe gasped at the sight and wondered what it meant. He knew most of what men and women did to each other from ugly experience walking in on Mom with her boyfriends and he knew babies didn't come from the stork. But if men put babies into women, it had to be better than this. The redheaded girl cried out when the doctor unplugged the pouch and something redder than blood sluiced down the hose, stiffening it as it flowed into the girl's bottom.

"It's cold," she whimpered.

The doctor clucked and chucked her under the chin. "Well, you'll warm it up, won't you?" He got up off his stool and slipped out through a part in the rubber curtains. Joe crawled like a ninja along the roof, peering in at any crack that leaked light until he saw something else.

Below lay a cavernous room with big tanks of water. The floor was deeper than the water level and waves rolled into channels cut in the floor, flooding the tanks through a Byzantine system of rusty pipes. The room was hot and dank, lit only by hooded crimson lamps.

A plank was laid across the tank directly beneath Joe's vantage point and a pregnant woman sat on a funny stool with a hole in the seat with her skirts hiked up around her waist. She strained and pushed like on the toilet. A huge man wearing hip waders and no shirt and a hooded fisherman's hat waded in the tank below her, but nobody else seemed to be concerned with her birthing her baby into the water.

The woman gave a piercing shriek and bent to clamp her head between her knees as she loudly expelled something from her girl-parts. The tank water was coffee-cloudy and simmering with tiny pink things like shrimp rolling around in it.

Other pregnant women sat in similar stools over other tanks, or lay on cots beside them, sweaty and spent from their labors.

Joe tried to move crabwise on the roof to see what was coming out of them, but the shingles gave way under his hand and he was falling through the roof. He threw his legs wide and caught a rafter, stopping his fall.

The hooded man in the tank looked up at him and grabbed a net on a long pole to drag him down. His torso and arms were carved up with deep scars like fissures in dry mud and all over his body, weird lumps and knobby lesions pulsed among his rippling, rangy muscles.

Joe swung his arms wildly, trying to lift himself up out of the hole in the roof. The boards trapping his knees groaned. The woman on the birthing stool howled and forced out something that splashed in the water. A turgid, translucent sac dangled out from between her legs, then ruptured like a soap bubble. Hundreds of finger-sized pink bugs spilled out.

Joe screamed, "Let me go!"

The man with the net swiped at Joe and banged his head, trying to drag him off-balance. The rafter beam under his left foot cracked and gave way. Joe squealed as he fell a whole foot, but something caught the waistband of his jeans and held him suspended over the tank. Around the big man's legs, newborn pink, spiny things darted and churned the water to a foamy stew.

"Quit fighting me, stupid boy!" Lorna's hissing whisper slapped Joe just as he was yanked backwards and rolled over the shingles to tumble off the drooping edge of the roof. He fell into an ancient shell-mound and rolled to his feet running. Lorna, with her long legs, was right behind him. Breathless, yet he kept screaming the same thing at her until she hissed, "Shut up or they'll come!"

"But that... that man... that was my dad!"

Joe rolled over and rubbed his eyes, but the dark got no lighter and whatever had awakened him did nothing to announce itself, but he felt clasped by the certainty that someone had been in the room only a moment before.

Crooked rays of tarnished silver moonlight leaked in through the shutters. The walls of the tiny bedroom seemed to sag even closer together. The crack in the ceiling pursed like lips whispering a secret.

A peculiar scent laced the air; salty and pungent like heated seawater, but richer, spicy, arousing. Pinned down under the stifling weight of the dusty comforter, Joe inhaled greedily. The heady aroma made him feel drunk and tweaked at the same time. His cock stood painfully erect, struggling to lift the heavy blankets into a tent. Rolling the covers back, he turned to the door just as the twin shadows of feet flitted away and something clunked on the warped floorboards just outside his door.

Cold hands probed his bowels. He hoped, and yet he dreaded, that it was Lorna. Playing her strange games. He couldn't figure her out, but he wanted her. Until just now, he'd been torn. Her games had seemed like naïve courting one minute and a teasing trap the next, snapping shut whenever he showed a flicker of interest. She was trying to draw him out because she was bored and he was an outsider, to make a clown of him. But he was bored too, and he had to admit she was pretty, if a bit odd-looking, with her wideset violet eyes, moonstone complexion and blue-black hair. At home, he would have noticed her, but never approached her, worried what people would say, because on the mainland, she would surely be a social outcast. She vexed him with her weird mingling of exotic beauty and deformity. Her weird, withered arm that she always turned away from him only seemed a minor distraction because she had tits like a cow, and Joe was a boy of thirteen.

But she was his cousin; it didn't just feel wrong the way stealing or drinking or smoking felt wrong, which was just the fear of getting caught. She was the strangest girl he'd ever met, but she was family. It felt unnatural, the way it felt when he caught himself staring at his mom when she passed out naked on the couch. And yet, the musky mist of her in the air still worked its magic on his brain and body, flatly showing him how very natural it was.

The fear of getting caught was no slouch in adding its voice to the argument, but Joe went to the door with no more hesitation. If this was another game, he'd play to win.

He eased the door open, careful not to let it bang into the bed, but this only drew the groan of the hinges out into a low bleat like a novelty cow-in-a-can. He jerked the door open, stepped around it, and peered out into the hall.

At the far end, a lantern cast a quavering orange glow from a niche beside Lorna's door, which stood open. The dark beyond the threshold was a curtain of soot, but he could nearly see the trail of scent she left behind and follow it.

Stepping out, he tried to remember which floorboards creaked and which of the several locked rooms lining the hall were occupied, but his feet wanted to carry him sprinting to the end. He took a step, planted it gently, was rewarded with a tiny squeak as if he'd crushed a mouse.

What did she want? What did *he* want, for that matter? He'd made out with a few girls from school and summer camp, had got as far as a quick furtive handful of bush twice, but this wasn't seven drunken minutes in a closet.

Should he whisper her name, or just go in? The prospect of going back to bed never had a chance. Fantasies raced through his mind and tied his cock in knots. If this were a game, he was not a player, but a piece.

A stirring in the dark continent of her bedroom and she appeared. In the somber light of the lantern, she looked like a woman, mature and ripe, though her eyes were hooded, her expression grave. She looked at the floor before him and parted her lips to run her tongue over them, slowly, savoring a taste on the air and sucked in a hungry breath that tapered off in a shudder of nervous delight. She might have been sleepwalking until just then and he figured he must look the same to her.

She gave no coy smiles, made no sound, no gesture to beckon him closer or send him away. He might not be there at all or he might be wrapped all around her, a maddening taste in the air of something that used them both. With her slender hands, she caressed her full breasts and the modest mound of her belly, the cello-shaped swells of her hips and down her thighs. At the limit of their reach, she began to gather up the folds of her flannel nightgown. Lorna's face contorted as if she were lowering herself into a scalding hot bath, but still her hands worked an inch at a time to unveil her feet, her long, coltish calves, her knees, her thighs—

Joe quivered. He dare not move. If he took a step, it would resound like a shotgun blast and wake the whole house, at least the ones who could hear. His heart pounded like a fist on every door in the hall. She wanted him, didn't she? She was in some kind of ecstasy, possessed to taunt him, but not enough to just steal into his bed. It was wrong; it was still incest, north of the Mason-Dixon line. He was getting sick of telling himself that.

Bereft of any script to follow, Joe just watched as she held the nightgown up around her waist. The unknown territory below was steeped in shadow, but her pale skin cast a soft light of its own, highlighting the sparse spray of hair on her pubic mound, little thicker than a teenager's moustache. With her other hand, she stroked the gleaming flesh of her inner thighs and roamed hungrily around the cleft of her sex like it was too hot to touch. Her legs spread wider and her hips slowly gyrated, offering him a better view of herself. Lorna let out a rasping sigh of torment and forced her hands to creep over her burning sex and splay her nether lips wide open.

The shiny visceral pink of it promised him everything a man dreamed of, death and resurrection and revelation. It stared at him, dared him, and denied him. Her agile fingers kneaded the layers of pouting lips and darted in and out of her fundamental hole, slathering her juices up and down the canal of her vagina, then trapping the pearl in the prow of her slit with her fingers and rolling it between them, her pouting lips clamped shut on a howl of ecstasy.

Joe's cock popped out at full mast through the fly of his pajama bottoms. Without a thought, he took hold of it and slid his hand up and down the shaft, squeezing it until the head burned purple and a droplet of semen oozed out his urethra.

Lorna's moans grew louder and higher. Her hand massaged the folds of her sex in a panic. Her hips jerked and bucked as if she were fucking him, urging him to redouble his stroking. Another second of this, and he would explode. He stalked down the hall with his cock in his hands like a dagger, stepping lightly but almost running headlong into her arms.

When he came close enough to touch her, it was like he'd broken a bubble, awakened her from sleepwalking. Her eyes went wide and she shrieked, "No, it's wrong, to touch!" and jumped back and slammed her door.

"What the fuck is wrong with you?" Joe shouted at the door. "What kind of game is this, anyway?"

Only then did he remember that some of the sleepers all around him could still hear and he turned and tiptoed back to his room.

Sitting in the middle of the doorway where he must have stepped over it before, was a small, queer porcelain bowl on a saucer, like for soup, except it was empty, and instead of a spoon, there was a glass eyedropper. He knelt and picked them up, and almost dropped them. They glowed with her heat and reeked of her crazy-making scent. She'd rubbed her juice all over them and put on a show for him and approved when he put on a show for her, but then he'd broken the rules. The bowl was shaped sort of like a miniature bedpan, with a contoured mouth that curled over to prevent anything from spilling out.

He realised, with a twitch of shock, that he was meant to jack off into it. He looked at her door again as if he could see through it and into her. He noticed a door down the hall hung ajar and the too-white face of his grandmother watching him.

"Go ahead, boy," she said, "do your duty," and closed the door.

"But, we're family. It's not right."

They were on the boat, waiting for Uncle Tab to bring the nets down in the truck. Aunt Meg was waiting for the doctor to come see Aunt Amelia. The sun was still an hour away from rising, and most of the other boats had already gone out.

"It's not for my pleasure, stupid." Her stormy eyes overflowed. "I want a baby. If I don't, I'll have to wet-nurse next season, and most of the boys on the island are so inbred, they can't even make—" She stopped, furious with herself and with him, then hauled off and hit him.

"Is he bothering you, Lorna?"

A huge hand like a catcher's mitt fell on his shoulder. Joe threw his elbow into the big boy's gut. He turned and blindly swung his fists out and upward.

The boy was a head taller than him. The punch aimed at his jaw connected with his Adam's apple. The boy folded and dropped to his knees, clutching his throat. A sickly wheezing came from his mouth, like a broken machine. His face turned purple, then blue.

"How was that? Who's queer now, bitch?" Joe screamed.

"Get off him, he's choking!" Lorna jumped on Joe's back. Joe shoved the bigger boy off the boat. Still choking, the boy fell over the gunwale into the water.

A big fishing boat came barging up the harbor lane out of the hatchery's landing. Its wake sent the boat heaving and rolling under their feet. "Angus, get him, help him!"

Joe leaned over the gunwale and reached down for Angus's arm, which stuck out of the narrow channel between the rocking boat and the dock. The boat rose up on a swell and closed the gap like the blades of scissors on Angus's arm.

Joe was holding the hand when the boat crushed Angus's upper arm bone like a stale breadstick. The strong, callused fingers clasped his so hard that the nails broke the skin of his palm and then it was like he was holding an empty glove.

Together, they pulled Angus out of the water. He vomited and started breathing, but his arm was crushed, and flopped backwards on his body when he tried to kick Joe. "Jonah!" he gasped, again and again. The other workers jumped down from their boats and came running.

"Go," Lorna said. "They'll kill you!"

Joe ran down the dock and up the hill just as the rest of the village converged on the Myrick boat. Uncle Tab's truck pulled up. He waved at Joe as the boy ran past, up the hill and off the road across the overgrown yard of the empty Kinchloe place and into one of the winding canyons that carved the island.

He hid in a treehouse. He didn't know when he fell asleep, but he woke up in a cold sweat, still seeing the hooded man in the hatchery, staring up at him from a boiling pot filled with unborn children. His grim lantern jaw and button nose should have comforted him, for his father was alive and he was here. But when Joe looked into his wide staring eyes, like burnt-out headlights, he realized that he was utterly alone.

A flashlght beam pinned him to the spot. "Don't move!" said a low voice, but he unclenched when he realized it was Lorna.

While he ate the tunafish sandwich, she tried to tell him why. "When a farmer grows corn, he must labor and give it his blood and sweat, and in the end it feeds his family and he'll plant more corn. He serves the corn. It's no different here.

"When all the fish died, the island went hungry. But we were born here and weren't meant to leave. They came up from the depths some years ago and they were something new, out of something very old. Doc Kinchloe called them isopods—living fossils. We called them a miracle."

Their cycle was broken too, for while they fed on all sorts of deep sea life down there in the dark, they turned into cannibals when they came to the surface to spawn and devoured their own eggs, if they were not separated and farmed. So the island learned to live off the new bounty from the sea, but they had other troubles.

Generations of inbreeding had led to nervous conditions and defects, like the deafness and palsies and seizures. The isopods were scavengers that ate, among other things, tons of medical and industrial waste dumped in their benthic feeding grounds. But something they ate or something they always were or the divine hand of the Creator, had made them just a little bit human.

"That's right," said Aunt Meg. Her kerchief-bound head peeked over the wall of the treehouse. "I thought I'd find you kids out here."

"You can talk!" Joe said. "You were faking it!"

"No, dear," she said, "I'm healed." She lifted her hair and showed him a fresh incision just behind her ear. Something inside it squirmed. She flinched in pain, but her smile at hearing and speaking again more than made up for it. "That's the miracle. If God meant for us to live somewhere else, we would've been born there. He provided for us. The catch doesn't just feed us, Joe. If we look after them and give them a soft harbor, they can heal us all."

Joe looked to Lorna, who lifted her shirt. He'd seen more of her than anyone already, but the sight of her breasts was not what he'd hoped. A livid pink bump on her collarbone, the size of a baby's fist, trembled when she touched it. "I was born with a bad heart. They put them in me... or I would've died a long time ago." With her slender body between Joe and her mother, she slipped something into his hands and flared her nostrils at him until he put it away.

Joe looked from one to the other, his mind reeling. It took him a little while to form a coherent question. "But if this is all so normal and natural, where's my Dad? Why is he hiding in the hatchery?"

Aunt Meg looked shamefaced for the first time. "I'm sorry about that, but you couldn't know about him, if we didn't know about you. Your father has a very important job. After all, he was the one who showed us how to use them."

Aunt Meg stepped aside and someone else came out of the dark behind the flashlight. Long, rangy arms reached in and grabbed Joe by the lapels of his jacket and jerked him out of the treehouse.

"We didn't want to keep him a secret from you, Joe, but you have to understand. He never really cared about family or about having a home. He hurt people here and tried to leave, but he had an accident and everything turned out for the best. He's... different, now. Don't expect too much..."

Joe kicked and screamed in his father's arms as the big man carried him out of the canyon. He knocked the hat off his head and all the fight went out of him. Joe's Dad was still Joe's dad up to his eyebrows, but his skull was a yawning, broken dome, filled to overflowing with something else.

An articulated shell, purple black with mottled pink spots, squeezed into the gap. It looked like a cross between a giant woodlouse and one of those prehistoric crab-creatures, a trilobite. Jointed legs with vicious claws scuttled and twitched against its underbelly, and its stubby lobster tail coiled and uncoiled out of the gaping wound, but its head was tucked in behind the mask of Sam Myrick's face.

Like a hermit crab in a deluxe human shell, the thing looked out of Dad's eyes at Joe as it carried him down to the docks, but was it really making his father's lips mouth his son's name and say, *I'm sorry?*

They went down to the cove, where the whole village waited. The women were out on the water in three long rowboats. They had dragged an enormous net across the width of the cove and now they sat at their oars and drummed on big tubs, a slow, pulsing dirge that reverberated through the water and the shore. The large fishing boat lay anchored in the center of the cove, with all its engines and motors shut off, a white island in the blackness.

The three dozen fit men and boys of the island raised a cheer and ran to their own rowboats when Joe's father came down onto the dock bearing his son like a trophy. The Clijsters, Rowbottoms, Blys, Smoodys and Myricks stood aside as Sam Myrick passed among them. Uncle Tab punched Joe in the arm and dropped a crusty lifejacket around his neck, but looked away and shook off his clutching arm.

The full moon peered over the headland, paving the black wasteland of ocean with a road of liquid fairy gold. No motors churned the water. The wavelets that slapped the sides of the rowboats were hushed and drained of force. The swollen tide was like an upwelling of infected, toxic effluvia from the depths, like the last, sour breath from diseased lungs: stifling and sickeningly warm, spiced with the narcotic reek of benthic decay.

Joe's father set him down in the prow of the first boat. None of the other eight young men in the boat looked glad to see him, except for Angus Smoody, who sat amidships and grinned at Joe. His arm looked no worse for having been crushed this morning, but for a jerking and twitching of each finger on his hand, one at a time, as if something were testing them. Bandages under his faded Blue Oyster Cult T-shirt wrapped his arm and chest, and covered a ring of squirming bulges around his shoulder and down his trembling arm.

He pointed at Joe once, then took up his oar. Joe had no oar. He turned around to look down into the water.

The cove rolled and sloshed in long slow movements, like a bathtub stirred by a vast, submerged body. Out beyond the point, the ocean was rent by frenzied slashing waves. The women raised a cheer and increased the tempo of their drumming.

The water was redder than blood, clotted with clumps of eggs like unripe grapes and chopped by sleek lilac shapes. Broad, armored backs broke the surface and grated the keels of the rowboats. The smallest of them was over three feet long and their jointed shells were crowned with spines like harpoons. Their blunt heads were fused with their thoraxes with two pairs of segmented antennae and four dull gray, sightless eyes. Jutting mandibles with sawtoothed ridges snapped out of mouths like garbage disposals. Recalling how few of the local fishermen had all their fingers, Joe drew back from the water.

A stiff arm shoved him over the gunwale and Angus's hot, whiskey-laced breath washed down his neck. "They come up from a mile down to lay their eggs and eat each other, little boy. They'll strip you to the bone faster than you can scream. And those are just the girls."

"Get off me, fucker or I'll hit you again." Joe looked from the redheaded boy's ruddy pug-face to the slack, vacant mask of his Dad. Mayor Smoody sat in the stern of the second boat, passing around a jug.

Angus laughed. "He won't save you." His injured arm jerked and dug its fingers into Joe's shoulder. "If somebody falls in, they come running and stay to feed and the catch is fat enough to last all year, isn't that so? What d'you say, boys?"

The men kept rowing, but they stared right through Angus at Joe. The moonlight made waxy masks of their faces, but none of them said a word.

On the crow's nest of the hatchery ship, old Ichabod blew a bosun's whistle. The mouth of the cove turned to foam. Sam Myrick stood up and silently pointed and the boats turned into the thick of the foaming water.

"Row, boys, row!" Mayor Smoody croaked. The bow dipped and rose, then began to bump and jerk as if they rode over a bed of boulders.

Joe leaned back close to his father, but he fell off the bench with the rocking of the boat. Angus laughed. The floor of the boat was filled with harpoons and spearguns. Joe grabbed a heavy iron rod, but the barbs cut into his soft hand and he dropped it.

The males were bigger. Hundreds of humped backs came pouring into the shallow cove. Their dorsal spines parted the water like shark fins. The red water turned to pink foam with clouds of creamy white discharge from the second wave of isopods. They raged and tore at each other as they fertilized the egg masses, then swept across the cove to attack the females trapped in the nets the women had set up across the harbor.

The nets were heavy gauge woven stainless steel. The smaller females streaked through its loose grip into the open sea, but the larger isopod cows were ensnared and easy prey for their mates.

The men towed the net across the mouth of the cove to trap the spawning isopods. Half dropped their oars and took up the drawstrings of the net, pulling it taut and closing the enormous mouth like a purse around the swarm.

Joe sat with his hands clamped to the bench, but he was ripped free with no effort at all by Angus's broken arm. "Clumsy Myrick, just like your dumb dad," Angus said. "You're gonna fall in."

Joe grabbed a speargun and swung it at Angus, who trapped the shaft under his arm. Joe's hand jerked it backwards, pulling the trigger. The spear whooshed out from under Angus's arm and passed over the heads of the other boys.

In the next boat, Mayor Smoody reared backwards with one hand resting on the thin spear where it sprouted from his solar plexus, and fell overboard.

The red water closed over him and came alive with teeth. A lifesaver was tossed. A man reached down, but something pulled him overboard, and the lifesaver was shredded before anyone noticed that Angus had thrown Joe out of the boat.

The cold, viscous soup smothered him, like wet plaster or half-hardened gelatin. Joe kicked for the surface. Something in his jacket pocket fizzed and flooded his nose and mouth with noxious bubbles. The packet Lorna gave him reacted violently with the water. When his head broke the surface, he was stained a bright yellow. Heart pounding the back of his throat, he reached out for the boat, gagging, "Dad, save me!"

The boat had capsized.

Thrashing bodies all around him screamed for someone to save them. The other two rowboats came abreast and threw harpoons and lifesavers, but the second boat overturned from wounded men trying to climb into it all at once.

Hands shoved him under the water as someone tried to climb on top of him. He fought them, but the arm he grabbed came away in his hand.

The water in his ears roared with the sound of motors, but it was the chattering mandibles of the isopods feasting all around him. His hands slid without purchase on the slimy hull of the capsized rowboat.

Something under him lifted him up by the seat of his sodden jeans. He curled up into a ball, no fight left in him. He was shoved up out of the water and thrown over the keel of the rowboat, and there he lay, clinging to the cold wet hull like a newborn to its mother while all the men of Quiet Island were slaughtered.

He saw only clasping hands and rolling eyes, peering up out of the red chowder. The third boat, filled with old and crippled men, was swamped by a male isopod the size of a VW Beetle with dozens of frenzied females boring into its bleeding exoskeleton.

When there were no more men in the water, the surges gradually subsided. The water around him was a thick, steaming stew of gutted isopods and human limbs. The rowboat turned and slowly, jerkily drifted to shore. Joe looked up and saw Lorna and Aunt Meg and Grandma Amelia on the sand, dragging the rowboat in by its dragging painter.

When he slipped off the boat in the shallows, he staggered, but Lorna came down and caught him. She led him out of the water, but pulled on him when he tried to sink to the rocky shore to rest.

The women were waiting for the conclusion of the festival. All the young ladies of childbearing age stood in a line, their somber eyes glazed with instinctual need. This, too, was a vital part of the catch, and the life of Quiet Island.

They waited with their eyedroppers and buckets for the men to come home.

LOST IN TIME

Steve Alten

The store is a converted garage, located on a track of land close to the beach on the outskirts of St. Petersburg, Florida. Hardwood display cases are stacked against the walls. Folding tables, covered in dingy-white cloth, divide the main room into three sections. On one table, a collection of Megalodon shark teeth, lead-gray and sharp, sit upright in plastic stands like six-inch stalagmites. Ammonite and trilobites share another table with jagged chunks of quartz crystal, the colored stones glittering beneath the store's bare light bulbs. Mammal bones and fossils from ancient Mastodons and ground sloths, camels and bison are displayed on the last table, along with bronze sculptures and bottles from the sixteenth century. Two racks of t-shirts and some original paintings complete the inventory.

Brian Evensen takes a deep breath, inhaling the musty scent of fossils and artifacts. The fifty-two year old divorcee registers butterflies in his gut as he wipes dust from an oak display case.

They're late. Par for the course...

He rubs the display case glass with a Windex-soaked paper towel, then lovingly rearranges the Indian artifacts he has spent more than forty years collecting from local rivers and construction sites.

The deep throttle of the Harley-Davidson bellows in the distance. Brian continues cleaning, his heart racing. He listens as the motorcycle turns into the gravel drive and skids to a halt beneath the neon-blue "LOST IN TIME" sign.

Bells jingle. A gust of wind carries a whiff of cheap perfume and tobacco. Brian inhales his ex-wife's scent, then turns to face her. "Hello, Dot. You look good. Maybe a little tired."

"We've been on the road a lot." She looks him up and down. "You lost weight."

"Prison'll do that for you. Where's the asshole?"

"Wade's outside and I doubt you'd have the balls to say that to his face." She strolls around the store, feigning interest. "When do you re-open?"

"Next week."

"Same ol' same old." She fingers a quartz rock, then looks up at the five-and-a-half-foot long sea creature mounted above her head. "Jesus, what the hell is that?"

Brian smiles. "It's a viper fish. *Chauliodus sloani*. Very rare."

"It's hideous."

"Yep. It's a deep-sea fish that migrates vertically up from the depths at night to feed. Most specimens are only a foot or two in length, this particular sub-species grows to almost six-feet."

"Its mouth reminds me of that monster in those *Alien* movies."

Brian positions a small step-ladder against the wall. He climbs up, unhooks the mounted trophy from the wall, then descends, laying the creature upon a tabletop for closer inspection.

Dot tucks strands of oily black hair behind her ears as she bends to examine the gruesome predator.

The body resembles that of a six-foot eel, its scales colored an iridescent dark silver-blue, its flank blotched in brown and yellow hexagons that reveal small light-producing organs. The viper's head contains large, bulbous, silver-rimmed eyes.

The most frightening feature is the fish's mouth. Hyperextended open as if unhinged, it contains needle-sharp, dagger-like fangs that are so large they cannot fit inside the creature's orifice while closed. Instead, they curve outward, running outside of the jaw. Two enormous lower fangs are so large, they would pierce the fish's glowing silver eyes should the mouth ever close.

Dot touches the point of a fang, drawing blood. "Ouch. You say these things stay deep?"

"Except at night. Wanna see something cool?" Brian points

to a long antennae-like organ trailing back along the body. "This is a light organ. The viper fish dangles it in front of its open jaws, flashing it on and off to attract prey. When an unsuspecting hatchet fish comes along. . . *wham*—the jaws snap shut like a steel trap."

"Lovely."

"See these brownish markings along the flank? They're called photophores—light-producing organs. Touch the fish and its whole body lights up. Neat, huh?"

"If you say so," she says, unimpressed, as she sucks blood from her wounded fingertip.

Brian stares at his ex-wife, the need to impress her outweighing his better judgment. "What if I told you this fish was only a juvenile? What if I told you I've unearthed evidence of a viper fish—as long as a school bus—that roamed the Gulf Coast millions of years ago!"

"Is that why you brought me here? To impress me with your fantasies? You're not a scientist, Brian, you're a hack. A bum who wasted his life collecting dead animal bones."

She walks away, enjoying the effects of her barbs.

"Why'd you do it? Why'd you leave me for this bum? Was it the prison sentence? I know five years is a long time, but—"

"I would have left you anyway." She pauses to light a cigarette. "All you ever cared about were these stupid relics."

"I was an academic! It's how I made my living!"

"Some living. We lived in a trailer."

"So instead, you left me and took up with the very asshole who sent me to prison."

"Don't blame Wade. It wasn't his fault the Feds nailed you."

"It was his pot!"

"You agreed to hold the stuff."

"Yeah, but you never told me how much. A hundred and fifty poundso... Jesus, Dot."

"I didn't come here to listen to you whine. You said you had a proposition for us. What's the job and how much does it pay?"

"More than even you can spend. Go get the genius and we'll talk."

She heads for the door, then turns. "Are you carrying?"

"A piece? Hell no. I'm on parole."

"Raise your hands."

He complies, allowing her to frisk him. "I never liked guns, Dot. You know that."

"Prison can change a man. Even you." Satisfied, she heads outside.

Brian returns the viper fish to the wall, mindful of its teeth. *You're right, Dot. Prison changes everyone...*

The door bangs open, announcing Wade's presence.

The biker is a big man, six foot-four and a solid two-hundred-and eighty pounds. His hair is long and brownish-gray, tucked beneath a red bandanna. The handlebar mustache melds into a crop of whiskers. Tattoos adorn his exposed flesh, earrings dangle from both ears. "Okay, dipshit, you got two minutes."

Brian hobbles closer, the limp courtesy of a shank during his third month at Eglan Air Force Base Federal Prison. Reaching into his breast pocket, he removes the coin, then flips it to the bigger man.

Wade examines it. "What is this? Gold?"

"Not just gold, it's a Spanish Doubloon. The heads-side is a picture of King Charles III. Dates back to the late 1700s."

The biker re-examines the coin, but does not give it back. "Where'd you get it?"

"Found it in an underwater cave and there's plenty more. I located a huge treasure chest loaded with doubloons, but the damn thing's buried in four feet of limestone."

"A treasure chest?" Dot's eyes widen. "How much do you think is down there?"

"Like I said, more than you can spend. I'd guess a few million bucks, give or take."

Wade eyeballs him suspiciously. "So why do you need us?"

"Obviously, because I can't do it alone. It takes two to three people or one of you, to dig into the limestone and drag the chest out."

"Why should we trust you?"

"The question is, why should I trust you?" Brian holds out his hand.

Wade pauses, then returns the coin.

"Before I went to prison, I worked as caretaker in the

museum at the Ponce de Leon Mineral Springs Spa in Sarasota. It was a long commute, but the owners loved me."

"Go on," the biker says.

Brian limps over to a heavy display case and removes a rolled-up geological survey map from a hidden drawer. He unravels it, spreading it out across the glass counter top.

"This map details the area. As you can see, the mineral springs is a sinkhole that descends in the shape of an hourglass. Visitors are allowed to wade along the perimeter of the lake, but are forbidden beyond the ropes. The ropes cordon off the rim of the sinkhole, which drops two hundred thirty feet straight down. The sinkhole probably leads to an ocean-access aquifer, but there's a huge cone of debris that blocks the way at the center of the hourglass, making the extreme depths inaccessible. About forty-five feet down is a series of caves. Ten thousand years ago, at the end of the last Ice Age, the sea level was much lower. Early man lived in these caves, leaving behind huge fossil deposits, which were excavated on a limited basis throughout the 1970s. All excavations were eventually called off after an NBC broadcast turned it into one giant Geraldo Rivera fiasco—"

"Enough history," Dot interrupts, "tell us about the gold."

"Pirates used to raid ships all along the Gulf of Mexico. Crews must've buried their ill-gotten booty in these caves. Easy for the archaeologists to miss it. Only reason I found it was because I was using a very high-tech metal detector."

"Thought you said there was no more excavations?" Wade asks.

"I told you, the Spa owners love me, they let me dive the caves on weekends. I'm the only one who knows about it... 'cept for you two."

Dot claps her hands. "We split everything three ways."

Brian shakes his head. "I get half. You two lovebirds can split your half anyway you'd like."

The biker strolls around the store, pausing every few seconds to fondle a fossilized shark tooth, messing up each row he touches. "When do we do this?"

"Tonight. The Spa closes at five. We'll come through the woods sometime after midnight. I've got a rowboat stashed in the foliage and my van's loaded with scuba gear and digging equipment. By sunrise, we'll be rich."

The biker approaches Brian. Places a heavy paw on his shoulder. "We'll go. But if you're lyin', I'll skin your bones and make you one of your exhibits."

***

The Springs International Spa, located halfway between Ft. Myers and Sarasota, Florida, is the second largest warm water spring in the western hemisphere. Over nine million gallons of naturally-heated water pump up from this mammoth sinkhole every day, the mineral content exceeding that of more renown spas in Baden-Baden, Germany and Vichy, France.

Privately owned, the Springs is now the centerpiece of a European-style family resort. Hundreds of tourists visit the Spa each day, taking therapeutic walks around the roped off perimeter of the lake, enjoying a massage, visiting the café and museum, or just sunning themselves along the sloping grass-covered banks.

The park opens at nine AM and closes at five. The last maintenance worker leaves by eight o'clock.

***

Brian parks the van along the edge of a thick wood. A dark blanket of Australian pines stretches high overhead, the trees blotting out the stars. Crickets chirp. The forest rustles.

The three treasure hunters exit the vehicle, then methodically unload the diving equipment. Buoyancy control vests and weight belts will be worn, tanks of compressed air, fins, and masks must be carried. The biker adds a heavy satchel of digging tools and a metal detector to his load. Brian slings an underwater backpack of lights over his shoulder, then leads his companions through the woods.

Guided by compass and flashlight, it takes the trio thirty-five minutes to reach the edge of the private lake.

The grounds are deserted, the night air heavy with sulfur.

Leaving their gear, they return to the woods for the rowboat, which Brian had left hidden beneath a fallen tree. Twenty minutes and fifty pounds of gear later, the three find themselves rowing the boat toward the center of the deserted lake.

They approach the middle of the springs, the scent of sulfur rising at them in waves, the bubbling heated water beckoning. After a few minutes Brian stops rowing, the boat now positioned above the ledge of the one hundred seventy foot in diameter sinkhole, its surface percolating with mineral flow.

"This will do. I'll go down first and secure the anchor inside the cave," he says, rubbing saliva inside his mask. "The pirate's chest is located at the rear of one of the caves, buried a good four feet down. Wade, you and Dot will dig first while I hold the lights. We'll switch every five minutes to preserve air. Once we access the lid, you'll pry it open with the crowbar and we'll empty the doubloons into satchels. The whole thing shouldn't take us more than half an hour."

Brian dons his swim fins and climbs overboard, careful to minimize his splash. Securing his face mask, he flicks on his underwater light, then instructs Wade to hand him the rowboat's anchor and metal detector.

Brian takes a last look at the stars, then places the regulator into his mouth and releases air from his buoyancy vest, allowing the anchor's weight to drag him below.

Wade waits until Brian's light disappears into the murky depths before strapping the four inch dive knife around his right ankle. "Once we get the gold, I want you to surface. I'll take care of your ex."

Thirty feet below, Brian falls feet-first into the sinkhole's depths, feeling the rush of hot mineralized water soothe his aching muscles. He stays close to the limestone wall, adjusting the air in his buoyancy-vest to slow his descent, his heart pounding in his chest.

Can you hear me? Can you feel my pulse reverberating in the water? Be patient, my friend. Be patient...

At forty-three feet his underwater light reveals a ledge that rings the hourglass-shaped sinkhole and the first of its shadowed recesses. It takes Brian several minutes to get his bearings. Following the ledge counterclockwise, he descends another twenty-two feet, then aims his light into a rocky orifice.

The narrow cave entrance cuts into the limestone like a shark's mouth. Brian secures the anchor inside, then swims into the hole, mindful of the stalactites, careful not to disturb too much silt. The familiar feeling of claustrophobia returns. He wonders if Dot will be able to handle the nerve-wracking sensation.

Twenty feet in, Brian's metal detector lights begins blinking rapidly, indicating the location of the buried object he seeks. Using the edge of the metal detector, he traces a rough two-foot square in the sand.

The cheese is in place... now to summon the mice.

Moving out of the cave, Brian rises slowly through the sinkhole, allowing the bubbling current of buoyant mineral flow to carry him topside. He surfaces next to the aluminum rowboat, grabbing onto the side of the vessel for support, spitting out his regulator. "It's all there, exactly as I left it. Visibility's a bit rough the first twenty-feet down, then it clears. Once we're inside the cave, try not to use your fins or we'll have silt everywhere. Hand me the tool bags."

Wade complies, then jumps in feet-first, followed by Dot. The two surface, oohing and ahhing.

"Shh! Someone might hear you!"

"The water feels so good," Dot squeals. "Wade, we have got to come back here after this is all over."

"Anything you say, babe. Maybe we'll buy this dump."

Dump? Brian grinds his teeth. "Okay you two, we gotta dig it up before you can spend it." He replaces his regulator and descends, using the anchor's rope to lead him below.

Dot and Wade surface dive, following him into the eerie depths.

The hot current presses Brian's mask to his face, the rising curtain of minerals tickling his flesh. His pulse pounds in his throat, matching the pressure building in his ears. Fear and adrenaline course through his body.

The fossil collector has waited five long years for this moment.

Five long years...

Sixty months. The words echo in his brain just as they had the day the judge spat them.

Two-hundred and sixty weeks, confined in a four by eight prison cell.

Eighteen-hundred and twenty-six days...

Brian shakes his head, clearing his thoughts. He knows the biker has no intention of allowing him to leave the cave alive, physically he is no match for the bigger man. Part of him had wondered if Dot still cared, but he knows now the love is gone—assuming it ever really existed in the first place.

She used you, just as she's using him. Heartless bitch.

Brian refocuses his thoughts, his eyes searching the depths from which the mineral water flows. *Can you taste our scent polluting your habitat? I bet you can...*

He reaches the cave entrance and slips inside, then moves quickly to the squared-off mark along the cavern floor. Gently, he situates himself in a kneeling position over the buried metal object and waits for his guests.

His mind drifts back to the first time he had dove the caves.

Twenty-two years ago... fresh out of college, job offers waiting. There were two digs that wanted his service. He would have killed for either job, but then he had seen that damn cave drawing and everything had changed.

Seventeen years of research... fueled by one chance encounter that had led to a dozen more. How he had yearned to go public with his information... the discovery of a new prehistoric species—the apex predator of a food chain anchored by the presence of chemosynthetic bacteria. The local Indians had taught him how their ancestors had lured the big ones to the surface—and Brian had learned his lessons well.

A light flickers from the cave entrance. Brian's heart skips a beat. *There are all sorts of treasures, Dot. Freedom is a treasure. So is revenge...*

Wade drags Dot inside the narrow slit, pulling her forcefully by the arm. Brian's ex-wife twists within the biker's grip. Underwater spelunking can unnerve even the most experienced diver, and Dot is just a novice. Surrounded on all sides, the sensation of claustrophobia overwhelms her and she panics, kicking at the big biker, forcing him to release his grip.

Dot darts back towards the entrance, churning up clouds of silt in her wake.

Brian shines his light through the debris as Wade emerges... alone.

Damn her! This complicates things...

Brian shines his light on the square in the sand, offering an enthusiastic 'thumbs-up'.

Wade nods. Takes the pickaxe from the smaller man and begins hacking at the limestone.

Brian's chest pounds like a timpani drum as his right hand steadies the flashlight... his left casually reaching between his legs... his fingers digging in the sand... searching until they feel the crusted rusty edge of the ancient anchor chain—leading to the brand new open steel shackle he has attached two nights earlier.

His eyes focus on the tattooed flesh of the biker's left ankle. *Now!*

Concealed behind a cloud of silt, Brian pulls the shackle free of the sand and snaps the open hinge around Wade's ankle, registering the gratifying *click* as the mechanism locks in place.

For a moment the two men lock eyes and then the fossil collector kicks for the exit.

Cat quick, the big biker wheels around and grabs Brian by his foot, dragging him backwards through the water, driving his knee into the base of the smaller man's back. Pinning him down, Wade's free hand reaches for his unshackled ankle and the dive knife.

Pinned chest-first along the sandy limestone floor, Brian struggles like mad to free himself from the biker's weight. He screams into his regulator as a burning pain sears the flesh behind his shoulder. A cloud of white silt blinds him, his blood swirling in the debris.

Wade stabs again. Misses.

Desperate, Brian twists around to face the biker, clawing at his face, flooding the biker's mask and blinding him, forcing him to let go.

Brian crawls and swims out of the biker's reach, then turns, watching Wade as he attempts to clear his flooded mask. *One down. Gotta find Dot!*

Groping in the darkness, he makes his way back to the cave entrance. Gripping the anchor's rope, he kicks for the surface.

Looking up, he sees Dot's silhouette. His ex-wife is still in the water, relaxing in the mineral flow as she holds onto the side of the anchored rowboat.

Brian surfaces next to her, spitting out his regulator. "Dot, we found it, it's all there! We need your help!"

"Forget it. I'm not going back inside that hole. The two of you can handle it."

"You have to come! Wade... he's trapped! His ankle, it sort of wedged between the hole and the treasure chest and I can't free him. Dot, we need your help!"

She looks at him, suspicious. "Since when were you so worried about Wade?"

Blood in the water... got to move! "You're right. Fuck him. Fuck that bastard. Let him drown. More treasure for us, right?" He replaces his regulator and descends ten feet, waiting to see if she'll join him.

Too frightened to follow, his ex-wife remains on the surface.

Time's running out, do something! Remember who set you up. She's just as guilty as he was. Do it now—finish it!

With a sudden burst of speed he resurfaces behind her, his left hand yanking back on her mouth, exposing her throat to the serrated edges of his blade and five years of pent-up anger.

Blood gushes from the mortal wound as Dot falls back against him, her strength draining as she thrashes against his chest.

Brian holds on, waiting until the last gasp of life fades into silence. Then he releases the air from her buoyancy-vest and drags her below.

Still too buoyant... Wait! The anchor line!

Wrapping one arm around his ex-wife's gushing corpse, he quickly cuts the anchor line and ties the loose end around Dot's waist. He leaves her there, suspended in death, the slit in her throat opening and closing like a second mouth as it releases blood into the upwelling stream of hot water.

Brian follows the line down to the cave. Balancing on his fins, he jerks the anchor away from the limestone and tosses it over the cavern ledge.

The anchor plunges into the darkness below.

Shadows dance along the near wall. He spins around confronted by Wade, the knife poised, the severed shackle dangling by his leg. The big man reaches for Brain, then pauses his eyes widening as Dot's carcass plunges feet-first past the cave entrance before disappearing from view.

Pushing Brian aside, Wade goes after her, his powerful legs pumping and kicking.

Brian's first impulse is to flee. He stifles it, then calmly removes the underwater flare from his pouch. He pops off the end, the burst of pink light nearly blinding.

Feeding time, my friend. Come and get it...

Releasing the flare, he watches it flip and spin, neutrally buoyant in the rising current, its iridescent beacon illuminating the geological funnel of limestone, its flame appearing like a bioluminescent lure to the prehistoric species dwelling one hundred fifty feet below.

***

Thirty feet below the cave and almost ninety feet from the surface, Wade manages to snag a fistful of Dot's dark hair. Kicking hard, he slows their descent, then pulls her into his arms—

Dead...

He releases her, his building rage suddenly stifled by the sight of the creature rising from out of the darkness!

The silvery viperous head is as large as a Volkswagen Beetle, its bulbous opaque eyes, glowing pink from the flare's flame, as wide as dinner plates. Curved, needle-sharp fangs— each as long as a toddler, riddle a mouth that seems to unhinge as it opens engulfing Dot's remains in one gruesome bite!

The iridescent dark silver-blue demon shakes its skull, the lashing movements slicing its meal to fleshy ribbons while revealing its tapered forty-three foot long body to the terrified biker. Covered in hexagonal pigmented photophores, the predator's hide blinks on and off like lights on a Christmas tree its sensory-laced scales detecting the presence of another.

Skin tingling, Wade inflates his buoyancy vest and races to the surface.

***

Brian's head bursts free of the hot spring and into the cool night air. Gripping the side of the rowboat, he raises one leg out of the water and with his last ounce of strength, pulls himself out of the water as Wade's hand emerges and latches onto his left ankle in a bone-crushing grip.

Brian twists around, kicking desperately at the freaked out biker as the rowboat begins to tip over, the night suddenly splattered with blood.

Brian falls backward, slamming his head against an oar. Dragging himself onto his haunches, he looks overboard, his heart fluttering in his chest.

The sinkhole is a frenzy of light and teeth and blood as Wade's lower body disappears down the massive gullet of the monstrous prehistoric viper fish, its bizarre set of lower fangs impaling the biker like a pair of eight-foot-long curved stilettos.

Wade flails in a cloud of his own blood, his cries for help muted by the water, his throes stifled by a sickening crunch as the creature's hyper-extended jaws snap together upon his cervical vertebrae. The biker's decapitated skull floats free, bleeding and spinning in the percolating hot mineral stream.

The viper fish feasts on Wade's remains until its gills flutter and its photophores cease blinking, forcing a hastened retreat to its sulfurous, deepwater purgatory.

Locating a fishing net, Brian leans over the side and scoops up Wade's bodiless head, the ache in his shoulder vanquished by an exhausting wave of elation.

***

"Welcome to *Lost in Time*, the most unique fossil store in Florida. How can I help you?"

"Just looking, thanks." The middle-aged man and his pregnant wife walk past Brian, pausing to browse at the rows of prehistoric shark teeth.

"Those are Megalodon teeth, fifteen million years old. Big shark, sixty to seventy feet. Everything grew bigger back then. We also have giant sloth remains and mastodon teeth. If you folks need any help—"

The man nods politely, then continues on. Pauses. Chuckles. "Hey hon, check this out. Wouldn't this make a fabulous conversation piece for Jack's office?"

Situated on a shelf beneath the mounted viper fish is a human skull.

"Like him?" Brian limps over and picks up Wade's freshly boiled skull.

"Is it real?" the woman asks.

"Hell, yes. Found it years ago at the bottom of a hot spring. Indians sometimes selected a white explorer as a sacrifice to one of their gods. God only knows how long it was down there."

"It's creepy," the woman says.

The man smiles. "How much?"

"Hundred bucks."

"I'll take it."

"What on earth for?" his wife asks.

"It's for Jack, you know, to congratulate him on his new job."

The woman grins. "He'll love it."

"Who wouldn't," Brian says. "Will that be cash or charge?"

"Charge. Do you deliver?"

Brian shrugs. "If it's local."

"It's local. Drop it off at Jack Morefield's office."

Brian grabs a pen and paper and jots down the information. "Jack Morefield. Where's he located?"

"Right next to the courthouse. He's the new District Attorney."

THE FISH THING

GUY N. SMITH

Leo didn't really want the goldfish. Indeed, he couldn't understand why he'd gone to the air-rifle range, or even the fairground, in the first place. Possibly, he thought it would take his mind off things. Off Mandy, that was. Air-guns held a morbid fascination for him... he stood there, a vacant expression on his face, clutching the jam-jar with the fish swimming about in it, and then everything flooded back to him.

That balmy August evening, walking through the sweet-smelling pinewoods, the air-pistol dangling loosely in his left hand, his right closed over the girl's. She was beautiful. Barely eighteen, with raven hair falling below her waistline, small perfectly moulded breasts visible beneath the half-unfastened blouse, her dusky skin and gold earrings giving her the appearance of a gypsy. Leo knew that she had Romany blood in her veins, that she came from the caravans parked way beyond the village. A tinker's daughter, but nonetheless attractive for it. The villagers had raised a petition to try and move the caravans. They'd surely lynch him if they knew that he was meeting one of the hated breed, making love to her in the woods every evening... or was it the other way round? She held a strange fascination for him, like a rabbit experiences when it comes face to face with a stoat, content to stand there and have the blood sucked from its veins. In his heart he knew Mandy only wanted his body, but he tried to convince himself that it went deeper than that; that she wanted Leo, the wandering farm boy who wandered from sowing to sowing, harvest to harvest, here today, gone tomorrow.

Eventually, they had arrived in the clearing which held the Pike Pool, a deep marl hole, its brackish waters hidden beneath a thick green scum of algae. Its circumference was no more than twenty feet, the branches of the tall oaks all around it meeting, the sunlight barely filtering through for a few hours during the day. A sinister place. A place of death. A child had drowned there last summer and it was three days before they had managed to retrieve the body, the frogman saying that he hoped he never had to go down in another place like *that*!

The old men spoke of the pike in hushed tones. A monster. He'd been a fearsome brute in their young days, almost pulling Abe in when he'd hooked him way back in the twenties. Fortunately for Abe the line had snapped. The pike had grown over the decades and on still evenings a ripple beneath the scum would mark the place where he lay, patiently waiting... for what?

It was because of the pike that Leo had brought Mandy to the pool. He wanted to impress her, do what other men before him had failed to do. They would sit on the bank in the long grass, the air-pistol fully loaded. A close range shot and there would be no mistake. The brute would float dead on the surface, they would pull it into the side with long branches and then carry it in triumph down to the inn, Mandy by his side. He'd be a hero in everybody's eyes, most of all Mandy's. Fantasies? The cold steel of the gun in his hand told him that it could so very easily become real.

Yet, it hadn't worked out like that at all. There had been no sign of the pike and after half an hour, Mandy had become impatient. Her thoughts had turned to other things, and as he bade her to be quiet, she had taunted him.

"You are a stupid boy!" her loveliness was transformed to bitter evil rage in a matter of seconds. "You think I am in love with you, eh? I love no man. Men love *me*! The foresters and the road-workers. They give me what you would never be able to give me if you lived to be as old as the pike. You have nothing. Not even guile. That fish laughs at you just as I do..."

It was at that point that he had shot her. One slug between the eyes was all that was necessary. She was dead on her feet, balancing there on the edge of the scum pool, her glazed eyes meeting his, and holding them. A few seconds that seemed an eternity, an expression on her features that was not even surprise. It was twisted evil that thirsted for revenge. Slowly, her legs buckled, and she slid, rather than fell, into the Pike Pool, the algae parting to receive her, and then knitting together again after she had gone. There had not even been a splash.

Leo had stood there for a long time afterwards. He did not panic. He was not sorry. She had got what she had asked for and he was satisfied. Then, pitching the empty pistol in her wake, he had set off back to Bastaple's farm in the gloaming.

There were no enquiries. Every day he awaited the coming of the police, maybe even the gypsies themselves, seeking the missing Mandy. Nobody came. The barley crop was harvested and by the time the fair came to the village he had ample time on his hands. There was little to do in the evenings in Clungunford. His mind was filled with hate towards the dead gypsy girl as the days passed. Indeed, he was almost tempted to return to the Pike Pool to gloat. Then he won the goldfish on the shooting range and that changed everything.

The more he looked at the goldfish, the more it reminded him of recent events. Its eyes saw him and returned his stare. It had the beauty of Mandy, the grace and the poise, but there was something else... a kind of superior bearing. Like the pike in the pool, it was a prisoner in its surroundings, yet it did not fear him. Instead, it seemed to mock him. 'Guile', Mandy had described the pike. Well, this goldfish had guile.

As he slept in the loft above the hay-barn, he tossed restlessly. Twice he was awakened by nightmares that found him in a cold lather. It was always the same. Mandy, the pool, a fish eating off her body in the thick mud at the bottom. It wasn't the pike, though. Well, not quite. It was big, fearsome, but bright orange in colour with eyes that seemed to bore into his brain. It was driving him mad!

Leo knew that he would have no peace until he got rid of Fish, as he had named his pet. In the cold sober light of a new day it seemed only too simple. The drain was the best place, entomb it in the sewers! No, that was too easy, he decided. There was a much better way. He would condemn it to the Pike Pool! He laughed to himself at the thought. It would have company. The Pike would pursue it relentlessly, but maybe it would escape for a time by hiding in the rotting corpse where the larger fish could not reach it. There would be several entrances.

The empty eye-sockets where the pike had gouged them out as a delicacy, the gaping mouth... and others. It would not starve. It could feed on decomposing intestines.

There was time to get up to the Pike Pool and be back in time for breakfast. Farmer Bastaple would not even know he had been away. So, he dressed hurriedly and started up the hillside at a shambling gait, some of the water out of the jar slopping over and wetting his shirt. He tried not to look at Fish. The thing was regarding him the whole time with unblinking eyes, a kind of smile on its face.

Leo jerked his head away several times. He felt almost hypnotized by the goldfish. It was almost as if it knew... and liked the idea! He was glad when he arrived at the brink of the pool. Glad because he could tip Fish in and get away. It was even more eerie in the half-light of morning than it had been that evening. It was more real. There was no atmosphere for idle daydreams and fantasies. He saw it as it was... a place of death, unknown terrors lying beneath the algae. One movement and it was all over. The scum barely parted. A few bubbles and then nothing. Flinging the empty jar away, he took to his heels.

It was two nights later that Leo awoke and knew that he had to go back to the Pike Pool. It had been in the dream that he had been summoned. That creature... pike or goldfish, maybe both... a Fish Thing, was calling him. Either he went up there and found his peace or else his mind would snap. What it wanted him for he had no idea. He had done it no harm. In fact, he had fed it... twice! Maybe it wanted feeding again. More victims, dead or alive. If so, then he would have to do its bidding. He didn't mind killing... not now, anyway.

Feverishly, he stumbled along the woodland path, trying to see his way in the faint moonlight which filtered through the foliage overhead. Several times he fell, wrenching his ankle, and tearing his flesh on wicked briars. It mattered not and he scarcely felt the pain as he dragged himself to his feet and staggered on. Soon he saw the Pike Pool. It was barely discernible in the deep shadow of the clearing, except that it was a darker shade of green. He pulled up abruptly on the brink, gasping for breath, and holding on to a gnarled and twisted oak for support.

The silence seemed to be pressing in on him. Not even an owl hooted. It was as though he were the only living being in the whole wide world... he and that Fish Thing down there in the murky depths. Then his nostrils wrinkled as they caught the stench. A foul odour that seemed to come from the very depths of Hades, maybe filtering up into this outlet from the River Styx. It was death and decay and something that was more evil than the mind of mankind could possibly hope to understand.

How long he stood there he had no idea. Perhaps it was a second, a minute, or an hour. Time had ceased. He was in a void where earthly dimensions mattered not. He had been summoned to cringe and to obey. It was cold. Not the cold of winter as he knew it, the crisp frostiness or the raw dampness. It was the temperature within his own body that was freezing.

He could see more clearly now. An ethereal light that radiated from no particular source enabled him to see every detail of the Pike Pool. The waters were stirring, the algae frothed and bubbled as the foul gasses escaped. Something was rising up out of the depths, something that generated an even greater coldness and brought with it a stench that was older than Earth itself. Evil incarnate!

Leo was forced to watch. He saw the head. A cruel pike-like face, the jaws, and the eyes glowing red. The most horrible aspect of all was its colour. A deep orange, its scales scintillating in the strange light which focused on the pool and nowhere else. The surrounding woodlands were an impenetrable blackness.

The vision changed before his eyes. The Thing seemed to shrink and then change shape. A human form, from the waist upwards where it emerged out of the slime, glowed a fainter orange. There was no mistaking the long raven hair, the perfect features, those gold earrings. It was Mandy. Alive. Risen from the dead.

"You fool," her words penetrated his brain, yet her lips did not move. Only her eyes glowed a deeper red. "You fool! You sought to catch *me*. Me! It is I who catch men. I have eluded them for longer than you can comprehend. You killed me with your pistol, yet you did not kill me. You do not understand? Then come with me and I will show you!"

Leo stepped forward, irresistibly drawn towards the apparition, feeling the water rise above his waist, up to his chest, and then only his head remained above the surface. The vision was changing back again. The fish-like head, the cruel jaws, a more pronounced orange.

Even the murkiness, as he went under, did not hide this Fish-Thing from him. With his eyes tightly shut he could still see it. Those jaws were open, waiting. It was then that he realized why he had come. The child last summer, Mandy, Fish, now himself. The Fish Thing would feast on his flesh and then it would become hungry again and its powers were not confined solely to the black depths of Pike Pool.

SHINERS

Michael Hodges

"Don't let it get the suction cup on your skin," John said.

"I can't help it, Dad," Eric said. "They are squirmy!"

John bent over, aiming his headlamp onto the boy's hands. A long, black leech squirmed between his son's thumb and forefinger. The leech tapped its sucker onto skin near the thumbnail, eventually finding a spot to latch onto.

"When it does that, when it exposes its underbelly like that, guide the hook right through the sucker pad," John said, adjusting his glasses.

Eric guided the brass hook through the sucker pad and the leech squealed. Juice from the bait bucket dripped down his hands as mosquitoes buzzed around their headlamps. Bats swooshed overhead, picking off insects that gathered around the light, their teeth hitting the insects with sharp, short taps. Inky water sloshed against the boat, and a lone frog cried out from the thick soup of vegetation near shore.

"Good job," John said. "Now gently cast the leech to the aft, towards those reeds. Try not to whip the rod or the bait might fly off. You could be sitting there for ten minutes asking yourself 'why aren't the fish biting' when the sad fact is the leech took a first class trip to St. Paul!" He patted Eric on the back and then moved out of the way, the boat shifting under his weight.

Eric stood, his thin frame unhinging like a colt. He lowered the rod behind him and then swung it forward with considerable gentleness. The glow-in-the-dark bobber twirled end over end, illuminating the peculiar flying leach with a green hue. A second later, the pleasant sound of the rig plopped into the water.

"Ok, nice cast, son," John said. "Now kill your headlamp so we can see the bobber. I didn't pay fifteen bucks a pop for these so we could chew up headlamp batteries."

"Gotcha, dad."

They turned the headlamps off and the world grew dark around them. After a few moments the landscape slowly brightened as the Milky Way set itself upon the sky with a subtle intensity.

The odor of fish and leeches permeated the air, a wonderful scent to serious fishermen. John and Eric glanced away from the bobber, to the tops of the red pine and hemlock on the shore—the silhouettes up against the stars.

"I like this dad," Eric said. "Will grandpa let us use this place more often?"

"Your grandfather and I have a sort of complex relationship, son. But I tell you what, he loves you to pieces and what you say goes."

Eric thumbed the handle of his rod, keeping it straight.

"Then I say another fishing trip next week!"

John smiled and turned around to take his own fishing rod. He unlatched the hook from the bottom guide, flipped on his headlamp and stuck a leech with the smoothness of a pro. He launched the bait to the edge of the reeds, using more force than Eric, but still retaining an air of gentleness. He switched off his light and they sat, two fishermen and two bobbers below the Milky Way.

"What the smallmouth like to do son, is they like to come up into these shallows at night to feed on minnows and crayfish. Our boat is right over a drop off. And this drop off rises gradually to those reeds. We are doing the right thing here, son."

John leaned forward and opened the small cooler, pulling out a chilled bottle of beer. He popped the cap, the freshness escaping with a frosty sigh. Eric could smell it in the clean air; he didn't care for it. He wished his dad didn't need to bring alcohol on their trips. Eric shifted in his seat and then relaxed.

The erratic wailing of a loon crossed the lake, making Eric think of places from a long time ago—things before he was born.

"Hear that loon?" John asked.

"I sure do. I hope it comes close to us."

"Well, not too close. We don't want a loon tangled in our lines."

Eric watched the bobbers undulating in the darkness, sometimes submerging to the tips, but never going fully under.

"Watch out for the walleye," John said. "They will peck away at your leech and get it off the hook without us even knowing it. They are lanky fish with solid white eyes and jagged teeth. If we can catch one, it will make a good supper—better than any smallmouth."

"Cool! " Eric said. "I want a walleye."

"You never know. We just might get one."

John drank from his beer and burped.

"You see son, it's about waiting these fish out. Technically, we are smarter than fish, but we are not in their element. If we were, catching them would be a heck of a lot easier. Up here, above their world we need to play the waiting game. And ain't it a pretty game with all these stars and trees?"

There was no need to answer. Only a goof would disagree, even at his age.

Eric glanced over to his glow-in-the-dark bobber. It was gone. He yanked the rod back with all his might.

"Set the hook, son! Set the hook!"

"I got it! I got it, Dad. It's hooked!"

The head of the fish jerked up and down, sending violent tremors through Eric's rod. The rod doubled over as the fish raced towards the boat.

"Good. Now apply just enough pressure. When you feel the line getting too tight, let out some slack by twisting the reel drag to the left, ok?"

"Dad... it's too heavy."

The rod bent in half again and line zipped off the reel. The smell of burning plastic rose into the air. Eric's rod thumped down, slamming into the boat, then straightened, then slammed down again.

"It's trying to go under the boat, son. Don't let it!"

"I can't dad! It's too strong." Eric grunted, trying to get position on the fish, playing it remarkably well. A sense of pride rose in John as he watched the boy play it out. *This is a damn fine fisherman*, he thought.

"Take the rod, Dad, I can't do it. Please take the rod!"

John stood behind Eric, reaching over his shoulders, holding the rod above Eric's hands.

"Okay, on the count of three, let go. One... two... three!"

Eric let go of the rod and they made the transition smoothly. John reached down to the reel and set the drag to the left, line still screaming out.

"Turn on your headlamp, then turn mine on, son."

Eric did as told and the night became theirs again, the Petersons out on the big lake.

John placed his legs apart, knees slightly bent. He held the rod high, not letting the fish get under the boat. *This might be a giant northern pike*, he thought.

John and Eric looked into the water, their headlamps shining into it, the slick blackness, the fine particles. The translucent fishing line cut through the water, the particles oozing around it.

"Get the net, son. The fish is tiring."

Eric stumbled to the back of the boat and took the cheap fishing net Dad bought from Jimmy's Bait n' More. His dad was poor and he loved him so for trying. Eric lowered the net just above the water, head scanning side to side, looking for signs of the fish. The surface roiled, revealing a bright-sided twenty inch fish.

"Wait a second—"

"This fish doesn't look right, Dad."

"Eric... go ahead and net the thing, I'm not sure what the hell it is."

Eric dipped the net into the water, the flowing nylon web ghosting around the shimmering fish. He raised the net, feeling the weight of it and laid it flat as possible upon the aluminum hull of the fishing boat. They looked down, hands on hips, mouths hanging open, their headlamps spotlighting the fish.

"What the hell?" John said.

"Dad, what's wrong? Is this bad?"

"It's not any fish I've ever seen."

The creature was long and sleek, with flashes of silver light streaking down its flank like a sign meant to grab attention. The head of the thing seemed to be missing and in its place were two peculiar eyes the size of billiards balls. The eyelids looked like those of an elephant; heavy, wrinkled skin and long, wet lashes. A short, skinny neck made of some unknown sinew connected to the football shaped body, then tapered off to nothing; no fins or tail of any kind.

"Dad... that light down its body, it's growing weaker."

"I see that. Don't get too close to this thing, okay, Eric? Actually, don't even touch it. We are treading unfamiliar ground here."

Eric stared at the thing, watching its abnormal eyeballs blink, the wet lashes now drying and sticking up into the air.

"We should put it back in the water."

"No... the professionals at natural resources will want to take a look at this. We might get our names in the paper. Hell, this could be a new species."

"Dad, if it is a new kind, we should throw it back and let it live. There might not be many of them."

Eric looked down at the odd fish; the flashing brightness on its side faded, then stopped.

"I think it died."

"Yup. Appears so—"

The creature began to croak loudly, the sound coming from the fat, fleshy sides where the luminosity used to be. It sounded like an amplified frog that had just swallowed sand.

Craaaaw! Craaaw!

"Throw it back now, Dad!" Eric cried.

"No, I told you we'll let the resource boys handles this. Don't worry about the noises. They will go away soon enough."

Craaaw! Craaaaw!

The bizarre fish shrieked louder, echoing across the lake, the sandy hoarseness of it.

"Dad, throw it back now! It's trying to live!"

"I'm not throwing it back. We've found something here. But I do know how to make it shut up."

Craaaaw! Craaaaw!

John raised his boot above the thing and prepared to step down hard when they both felt a warm rush of air. Eric's empty soda can blew into the lake, and his dad screamed; a sound he had never heard before.

Something in the air was trying to take his dad.

Eric heard flesh ripping. He turned towards his father and saw four horrible, silvery claws dug into each shoulder, pushing out streaks of blood through the blue long sleeve shirt. The headlamp reflected off the hooks which seemed to be curved, rough, clear plastic protecting thick, blue arteries. His father's eyes widened and his body lurched upward each time the claws dug into his shoulders. Gushes of air beat upon them, coming from wings that Eric could only see when he looked upward with the headlamp. Eric reached out to his father as another sky thing soared towards the boat. Eric ducked, making himself even with the gunwale.

"Dad!"

"Son... get to shore now—"

Before John could say another word, he was picked up from the boat and taken into the air. He screamed again, the sound muted randomly by the enormous wings of the sky things. The creature on the floor of the boat followed with its own scream, but it was different this time—a scream of joy and derision. The sandy croaking stopped.

"Dad!"

Once more his father screamed, somewhere in the night sky, not far from the boat. Eric followed the noise with his headlamp, catching a glimpse of fleshy wings pulled tight like a tent with fine, short hairs. Halfway down each wing a discolored, white hook jabbed out. He could hear flapping and gristle tearing.

"No! Dad, come back!" Eric said, crying.

The dismal wings flapped again and Eric heard thick, chunky liquid falling into the lake. Eric kneeled in the boat, huddling below the gunwale. With his ear almost to the aluminum hull, he heard what sounded like a heavily filtered concert; a sea of delightful screams. He slowly followed the hull rivets up, then peered over the side. Upon the lake, hundreds of shiny fish swam towards the surface, their lights shimmering with hyper-activity. They appeared to be heading in the direction where Eric heard the liquid fall into the lake. The first ring of loathsome fish splashed and crashed the surface like trout eating corn at a petting zoo pond—the joyous, filtered screaming accompanied by a violent, fleshy smacking noise. A vast numbness overcame Eric and he slunk back below the gunwale, huddling there, arms across his chest. He remained quiet for certain, unspeakable death awaited him if he slipped even once. The splashing soon faded and the night throbbed with the beat of leathery wings. Out behind him, towards the reeds a glow-in-the-dark-bobber rose and fell.

THE WORST THING EVER

Anthony Wedd

So, like, worst thing ever. *Another* forty plus day, how many was that in a row? Stuck inside in the aircon drinking endless iced coffees and ginger beers. I mean Philip and Marie are awesome, but there's only so much you can talk about without anything to do. At least we still had the cricket to listen to, which is cool for a while, like nostalgic or whatever, but I was leaving Adelaide on Sunday. If we were going to do anything it had better be pretty soon.

Maybe I seemed grumpy as I pushed my scrambled eggs around, or maybe Philip felt the same way, because he offered to take me out in the boat. Marie was like, "In this heat? You'll die," but I thought it sounded all right and Philip promised we would drown ourselves in sunscreen and wear like twenty hats. "It'll be cooler out on the water anyway," he said. Marie packed us a whole esky full of clinking bottles while Philip went out and got things ready with the boat. I changed into my bathing suit under an old t-shirt, just in case, and fumbled my cricket cap out of my sock drawer.

Outside it was already about a thousand degrees and I wanted to wilt as Philip led me over to the Land Cruiser and helped me up. The engine woke like a big growling dog, drawing breath at each gear change as we stop-started our way through the suburbs. In Melbourne play had started and we listened to it on the crackly AM radio over the roar of the air conditioner. "*Now it's McGrath coming in, he bowls to Tendulkar, angled down the leg side. Tendulkar fends it off his pads and there's no run.*" And repeat, again and again, all day. I love that shit though, what can I say, best thing ever. That *is* summer to me.

Philip stopped at a servo to get fuel and bait. He left the radio on for me, but play stopped for drinks and the news came on. There were bushfires in the Mt Lofty ranges. They were pretty bad—no one was dead but a bunch of houses were threatened. Some fire guy talked for a while. Petrol hummed and whirred into our tank. We got away just as play started again—Brett Lee was bowling, who everyone reckoned was like the hottest guy ever. I heard the clicking of indicators and we slowed and turned more and more often, approaching the beach.

Despite the heat, the boat ramp was like a mall, crowded with voices and boat engines. Hot wind gusted about my head as I stepped cautiously off the runner board. Philip paid the launch fee and bought me a Cornetto. I ate it sitting in the shade amongst fishy salt and exhaust fumes while gulls cawed and whistled. A panting dog yipped near me and I offered my fingers, but its owner was all, "Psst! Mindy, no. Come away."

"It's OK," I said, but they'd gone.

Philip came back and led me over wet, slippery rocks onto the ramp. I totally hate this part. I have to lean on him the whole way like some kind of invalid with every old fisherman in like a five k radius watching. I forced a giggle as he all but lifted me into the boat (so embarrassing), while the stale smelling ocean lapped and sucked below. The motor grumbled loud fumes as we started up and cruised slowly out of the marina. Finally Philip got me to grab the hand rail and we revved up and broke free.

All the noise of the world disappeared; there was only motion and hissing spray and the gurgling roar of the motor vibrating through my body. The sea was fairly choppy and our speed turned the waves hard. We bounced over them like beach balls, showering cold water, sometimes slamming into one like granite. I wanted to be like this for hours, speeding through the waves with my hair streaming and whipping in the wind. But soon the force of the motor dropped off and we eased into the swells, sloshing rather than fighting, as Philip neared his spot.

The anchor ground and clanked its way overboard. The world was back and I grudgingly accepted it by holding a rod for Philip while he messed around getting the bait ready. I could smell the wet stagnant flesh of whatever it was. He cut it up and

I could hear the knife sawing through soggy tissue before each finishing *thop*. Like, yuck. Silent jiggling as he baited my hook. Then the rod free in my hands, the hiss of casting, the *plop* of the sinker.

I tightened the line and concentrated. Fishing's best early on, while it's still novel or something and your hands aren't all gross. You could feel the sinker dragging along the bottom with each wave, a slow pull then relax. You'd also get nibbles, tiny fish gnawing at the bait without really grabbing it. Philip pulled the canopy over so we were sitting in the shade and turned on the radio. "*... final delivery of the over. Warne... pitches it on middle and off and Tendulkar is watchful, waits and lets it go outside off stump.*" It couldn't be long until lunch now.

Philip got me a ginger beer and we hung out listening and fishing. The canopy cut the sun enough that the heat was sufferable and there was still a bit of a breeze. After a bunch of nibbles I reeled in and felt down the line. Sure enough my bait was all gone. Philip thought it would be cool for me to bait my own hook. He handed me a cockle. Bait is just gross, you know? Like a chunk of limp rubbery slime that always wants to drip off your fingers. You don't want to grip it too tight or you feel like you'll pop one of the oozy bits and stink up your fingers even more. It's like living snot, or someone's insides. And somehow you have to get a hook through it and it's tough like gum. Disgusting.

Anyway I recast and almost straight away got a real bite, breaking through all the wishy-washy stuff with a sudden jagged jerk. Over the crisp clatter of the reel Philip was like, "Got him?" and I nodded. The distant weight of my fish pulled against me, twitching urgently through the line as he struggled. I stood up and reeled. Soon my fish splashed free of the water, line thrumming tiny droplets onto my face and arms as he continued to fight.

"It's a whiting. A beauty," Philip said and the line went slack as he grabbed the fish. He pulled my hand over and let me touch it. I felt the rigid triangular head, gills pulsing, then ran my fingers down the soft, slippery body. The fish wriggled, abruptly sharp with fins and I felt the soft crater of an eye knock against me as I snatched my hand back.

"Uh oh, bastard's swallowed the hook." Philip took the fish away and I heard its body drumming on the bait table in brainless bursts, the same violent fluttering rhythm as its bite. Then I heard the knife again, crunching scales and grinding through cartilage. I thought I heard the fish choking as the knife pressed deeper, or maybe it was gas escaping from some secret chamber or sac moistly popped open. "There we go," Philip growled. I couldn't imagine what he was doing and it was a bit gaggish, so I turned the radio up while he finished. The boat rocked gently rather than lurching like it did when we came out. I was over fishing for the time being. So when Philip touched my hand to press God knew what into it for rebaiting, I kept it closed and asked if I could swim instead.

He'd let me go off the boat before, a couple of times. Plus he must have noticed my bathing suit under my T-shirt and he hadn't said anything, so it was sort of already OK. There was this lifejacket that I wore, and we always clipped a rope to it so I couldn't drift away without noticing. So lame, but there was no one out here to see anyway. I stripped off while he got them for me, but he made me put *more* sunscreen on my newly exposed bits before I could go in. Whatever. I listened for the score off the radio while I did it—two for ninety-eight. Tendulkar had been dropped on forty-five while we were messing around with the fish. Worst thing ever.

Philip was like "lunchtime when you get out, OK?" and I was like, "Uhuh." Then he clipped the rope to me and held my hips as I climbed onto the side of the boat and balanced. This part was always a bit scary, but I didn't want to hang around up there in case a wave showed up and knocked me over, so as soon as Philip said, "Go for it," I jumped. I free-fell for a moment, then hit the water, shockingly cold to my warm skin. Submerged, all sounds were lost to churning bubbles, tangy stinging salt water trying to get up my nose. Then I bobbed to the surface, rising and falling. Philip was clapping, which was a bit cringeful; he doesn't usually treat me like I can't do anything. But I felt grateful and excited and gave him a breathless smile as I started paddling around. My latest thing was practising backstroke, which I'm pretty good at.

After that, I floated on my back for a while, arms and legs splayed. My ears went in and out of the water with each wave, exploring both worlds while the sun warmed and prickled my salty face. Philip started calling out to me, real loud. His words were kind of muffled by slopping water and my hair was in my ears too, but he was actually shouting, louder and louder. The rope went taut, like he wanted to reel me in. Something must have happened in the cricket, something pretty amazing. I rolled over and kicked myself upright.

"Wicket?" I called, wiping my hair out of my face.

"Shark!" he yelled back. What did that have to do with the game? Was it someone's nickname? I couldn't connect it with Philip frantically pulling on my rope, nor to the sound of tearing water like a big wave about to break behind me as a current pushed me forward and up.

A huge splash slammed into me like an explosion. I launched half out of the water but something clamped me like a vice from below. Boat? Jet ski? Oh God—shark—Philip had seen it. Droplets showered down like rain. Its mouth engulfed me—hips, thighs, everything down there—squeezing me like a pustule. I thrashed wildly and bounced off rock hard gritty flesh. I grunted as I felt it bite down, the pressure on my lower body immense and crushing. I couldn't scream; I could only gasp and try not to burst. Then I was underwater.

My head submerged without a breath, all sounds cut off except bubbles and rushing water. Without thinking I sucked burning salt water into my mouth and nose. I had to get away, right now. I had to breathe. We seemed to be going down forever. I was drowning. I squirmed and tried to kick, but my legs and stomach felt pressed like a flower. Something pulled at me from above; the rope, growing tight. The shark slowed and shook me in a violent spasm. I didn't feel any pain. It was just like a fish tugging on a line.

The shark lunged against the taut rope and suddenly I felt myself torn out of its mouth. I was free. Immediately I began to rise, swept upwards by the massive body passing beneath me. My lungs hitched; I wanted to inhale and take my chances, but the thought I might live kept me from doing so. I clawed at the water, desperate for the surface. How fast could the shark turn?

Please don't let it get me again. Not again. Please let it go away. Philip, get me...

I surfaced, raggedly wheezing warm brine from my mouth and nose. Philip pulled me backwards through the water, wailing my name in a frightening high voice I'd never known. I tried turning around, frantic to be back on the boat, but my numb legs wouldn't kick. Instead I groped backward so Philip could grab me. He must be close; I could hear his breathing now, hyperventilating almost. I wanted to tell him I was OK, but it was tough to get my breath, and I couldn't talk. I wriggled my fingers hi to him instead. Even holding my arms up was draining. But then he had me, his strong hands around my wrists, lifting me.

I came clear of the water, feeling the side of the boat scrape down my shoulders. Philip screamed, deafening, right in my ear almost. Was the shark back? He'd hesitated lifting me aboard and I tried to scream back at him, tell him to hurry, but I just couldn't get enough breath. He shrieked again, words so loud and jagged that I couldn't understand them. Then he was whimpering as he pulled me the rest of the way in and laid me down gently on the deck. He muttered a flurry of words between thick breaths.

"Oh-Katie-Katie-darling-oh-god-don't-move-you're-ok-don't-try-to—"

What was wrong with him? I felt faint, but that had to be normal. I was numb below the waist where the shark had cut off my circulation, which at least meant no pain yet where it had bitten me. Maybe there was a lot of blood down there where I couldn't feel. Frightened, I reached a wavering hand down to touch my legs, but Philip grabbed it.

"Don't do that honey, don't... just lie still for me. You'll be ok, I'll get you..."

He didn't want me to touch the bites. Whatever. He was sobbing. *Sobbing?* I wished I could comfort him. I really felt OK, just a bit weak and fuzzy. There *was* blood somewhere; I could smell it, thick and sour. That was OK, Philip knew first aid, though we'd probably have to go to the hospital. There was another smell too, heavier and grosser, like rotten meat. Probably the bait. I must be lying near where we kept it.

An alien noise startled me. A gull had swooped into the boat, I could hear it down near my legs, screaming and worrying at something. Phillip roared at it, thumping, his voice raw and crazy. He put a towel over my bottom half, kind of lifting me to wrap it underneath as well, and fiddling some more beyond where I could feel.

I was worried the shark would come back and attack the boat. They did that sometimes. My breath came in shallow gulps and warm salty water kept collecting in my mouth. With an effort I spat a bunch of it out and took the deepest breath I could, feeling pain in my chest for the first time.

"Is... is..." That was all I could whisper, but Philip heard me.

"Yes, sweetie, it's OK. Don't try to talk, just please lie still. We'll..." He could never seem to finish. He moved away and I heard the *zip zip zip* of the anchor rope as he pulled it in, really fast. Any second now I'd hear the chain snarling across the bow and we could go. I yearned for hospital and a warm bed. Despite the sun on me, I was getting cold. I'd have to stay way past Sunday. Maybe I'd have scars. I could be like a celebrity, the blind teenager who survived a shark attack. I might go on *A Current Affair*.

Surely feeling should be returning to my legs by now, a tingling or something. What if I was paralysed? A calm voice reassured me. Not Philip, someone else. I struggled to focus on it, everything sounded strained through cotton wool. "*Brett Lee. Bowls to Ganguly... wide outside off stump! Ganguly swings and misses, a big appeal! Not out.*"

Weakly, I lifted an arm and reached towards the towel. My lifejacket ended just below my ribcage and I started there, tracing down my stomach. It was dry and cool to the touch, and I felt my finger dip briefly into my navel. So far, so good. Then I met the towel. I paused there for a while, gathering courage, a fold of it between my thumb and forefinger. The commentators droned on, always relaxed. "*Definitely worth a shout there. I'm not sure there wasn't some noise... Certainly Lee thought he had him...*"

"Hang on, Katie darling, we're getting you home. Hang on." Philip's shadow fell across my face briefly, his voice hoarse with the effort of calm. He didn't seem to notice where my hand was. I slid a bit as he started the engine and slammed it straight into high gear, but I didn't lose my grip on the towel. A bubble of salty fluid formed on my lips and popped. My hand trembled as it loosened the sodden cloth above my right hip, exposing flesh smooth and cold to the touch.

I probed further. Where was my suit bottom? No wonder Philip had—abruptly my fingers smeared through something crusty, and my skin ended mid-hip in a jagged flap. I gasped, hissing like a punctured blowfish. Frantic horror sent my whole hand burrowing under the towel but I couldn't find my legs. The tear extended right across me. Below it was nothing but more towel, sticky and hideously limp.

Oh no-no-no, that couldn't be me.

Sounds dulled and merged into a single ringing tone. The sun and the hard deck melted together, squeezing my head like I was drunk. The shark got the rest. It ate me. Gorged on my chewed up legs and lower body. They were inside it now, losing their shape, coming apart in pulpy chunks you could squirt through your fist like rotting jelly. My feet were just bones now, fanning open like mucus-webbed fins. Eyeless fish heads swam in a stringy soup of my flesh scrap slime.

Philip shouted into the VHF over the smothered bellow of the motor, hysterical for both of us, and everything was real again. I slowly curled my fingers over the middle of my torso where I ended. The skin was thicker than I thought, spongy and rubbery like a tyre. I wanted to pull it down like a skirt to cover my insides. I gripped it feebly, fingertips slipping slightly inside my body. My knuckles touched some stuff that had spilled out of me.

I tried to scream and salty fluid geysered weakly from my mouth. Blood, it was blood, of course it was. Everything in me was fucked up. I couldn't be alive with stuff hanging out. Crying, I gripped the towel with my free hand and lifted it with a drawn out grunt. It came off me with a moist peeling squelch, scraps trying to cling, a faint pulling and shifting from inside me. The meaty smell I'd noticed before billowed out, raw and putrid. I convulsed with vomit but there wasn't enough left of me to arch properly. Instead I slid across the deck, slick with discharge, curling like a severed prawn. I banged into something and felt an ominous loose sucking from my lower torso.

Icy numbness crept up my belly. I shifted and gingerly worked my hand further into myself, trying to hold things in. Soft tubes and flaps of flesh squeezed and coiled together, as though I was a ruptured sack of fish. They jostled and squirmed, trying to get out of me, slipping through my senseless fingers. Sliding down the deck, drumming out their mutilated death throes in the stinking afterbirth. I had to stop them, put them back inside me. But there were so many.

I found I could move, chase them down the deck to where they were splashing overboard. Without waiting I dove into the chill water after them. As it enfolded me, the radio dulled and the stink of my open body faded. But I could clearly hear the chaotic vibrations of my quarries. I followed them downward in irregular thrusts, but they kept splitting into smaller and smaller schools, always leading me deeper. I pursued the largest group, following the flickering rhythm, but after some time I could count the number that were left.

One at a time they peeled away until there was only one, darting around, evading me. I was so deep now. I couldn't keep up. My freezing limbs stiffened and wanted to curl up for warmth. The only sound left was the tiny thrumming of my last fish, which became more and more distant. Fainter. Fainter. Eventually I doubted I could hear it at all.

THE KRANG

James Robert Smith

They claimed that there was a krang in Lake Dorr.

Because of this, Mangrove the City was holding its collective breath. In earlier times there would have been sacrifices made to appease the gods and to attract the monster itself. But Mangrove was ruled by less barbaric folk in these enlightened days. Now it was left to the work of the best men to rid the lake of the krang. Rewards were offered. Gold was to be paid—the highest of bounties.

Because everyone knew what would happen if the beast were not found and killed in all possible haste. It would first kill any unwary fishermen who plied the lake without proper care and without effective weaponry. And after that it would deplete the schools of fish that did so much to feed the burgeoning population of the expanding capital of Mangrove.

With speed the krang had to be located, captured, and killed.

If—Jove forbid—it actually spawned, then all would be lost. The lake would end up a dead and barren waste of sterile water. Merely that and nothing more.

The bars were packed because the town was filled with people having come from every city in the kingdom to try to earn the bounty for ridding the lake of the krang. Already several fishermen had vanished—and if anyone had doubted why, the wrecks of their crafts had washed ashore, one of them having the pearly white teeth of the awful creature embedded in the oaken planks left on the rocks. Someone who'd seen those teeth had held up his hand, indicating that just one of the ivory daggers was wider than his palm.

Hoggman liked that the bars were full. A full bar and crowded streets meant that he could beg enough spare change to put a roof over his head and food in his belly. If not that, then mead in his gut so that he could forget about his station in life. Hoggman was a beggar when you got right down to it. He wouldn't have called himself by that base and common term, but it's what he was. To hide from that label he liked to think that it was his yarns and glib tongue that earned him the odd silver piece that kept him from starving. In his darker moments, he would admit to himself that it was his crippled, withered left arm that made him an object of sympathy that put change in his purse.

And of course Hoggman made sure that one and all could see his deformed member. He wore his clothes just so, not hiding the weathered, stick-like ruin of a limb. No sleeves for that arm, no sir. More than once a sad-eyed sailor had been moved to tears and had emptied his coin-filled fist at Hoggman's feet. Or sometimes a lady would do the same, seeing him and wondering who cared for this poor beggar plying the streets and unable to fend for himself.

Aye, Hoggman had a withered arm and thank the gods for it.

That afternoon he had been moving up and down the docks, looking a few times for honest work and failing in that had turned to his storytelling and joking to coax some money or some drink from the men and women who made the shores of Lake Dorr if not their homes, then at least their livelihoods. The street along that waterway smelled not so much of fish as normal. Many of the fishing boats were tied up tight to their moorings or even pulled up high on the rocky beaches in case the krang mistook them for mates and tried to hump them into splinters. It had been said such things had happened when a lone krang found itself isolated in a strange body of water, waiting to spawn.

But the docks and the businesses along it were filled with people whose faces were lined with concern and with no room for laughter or, sad to say for Hoggman, charity. Instead, he saw anger in the familiar souls he encountered and hard stoicism in the eyes of the strangers who were streaming into Mangrove to hunt the krang. They didn't have time for beggars and they didn't feel like hearing a joke or an amusing tale.

So by the time the sun was setting in the west Hoggman found himself in The Whore's Bosom, one of the less inviting inns on the southern pier, but a place where he could sometimes depend on a free mug or three of beer from the owner, one Pearl, who had once been a comely prostitute who sold her body but who now—at the wise old age of thirty—owned the stinking inn and made her living selling drink and food and a warm place to bed down, generally without her as companion. Pearl sometimes felt sorry for Hoggman and would set him up with drinks, for he almost always repaid her in some way—either with coin when it came to him, or with some labor, for if he did have only one good arm, at least it was powerful, having to compensate for the worthlessness of the other limb.

That was why, when the sun was gone and the moon was riding the clear skies, Hoggman was screaming drunk, sitting in the midst of the bar, regaling one and all with stories of his days as a sailor and a fisherman. That was why he came under the sharp, clear eye of the outlander who was sitting still and alone in the shadows, his back to the stout walls, hanging on every damned lie coming out of Hoggman's drunken mouth.

"I have sailed Lake Dorr from end to end," he bragged. "I have seen the north of it where it comes to our borders with the barbarian nations in those cold regions." He'd scanned the faces looking up at him and down at him. "Yes, I have. Once I took a sailboat and the winds of summer led me far to the south where the lake spills down the Cane River until I came to the Dragon's Ladder where the rocks will tear a boat to bits." Smiling, he'd added, "And then I turned my boat round and sailed it all the way back. Aye!"

"What about a krang? Have you ever laid eyes on such?" Someone asked him. It was a young kid, fresh from the City of Mangrove, the capital, come down to the shores of Lake Dorr to do battle with the beast and earn the bounty that would make him wealthy.

In fact, few men had ever seen a krang. The monsters were not of the land of Mangrove and how this one had ended up in the lake was merely guesswork. Some said Jove himself had placed it there. Others that Gault, that nation of evil, had sent it to their Lake Dorr by way of some overland barge, depositing it in the waters where it would ruin the economy that supported this part of the country. There were pictures of the krang in books, but those books were in temples where only the monks and priests could see them. It was said that the sight of such a creature could drive a weak person mad.

Knowing all of this, Hoggman said the first thing that came to him. "Yes, I have seen the krang."

"Where?" It was as if every throat in the inn rose at once. The roar of it startled even a practiced liar like Hoggman.

"Not this krang," he admitted. "It was one in the Mungpo River, in Rama." He doubted any man there had ever seen Rama—one had, after all, to cross six borders to find it. "In my youth," he continued. "I was on a fishing ship, the Globe, it was—the hold could take on two tons of fish. The captain had been hired to find the krang that was ravaging the stocks along that shore of Rama and we did it. We landed the beast." Everyone was silent.

Hoggman looked to his left, eyeing the dark, useless bit of bone and skin that hung down to his waist. "It was how I came to lose the use of my arm," he muttered.

Looking up, he saw two-dozen heads nodding at him, believing. They were, after all, drunk to the last one of them. After that, the drinks came to him one after the other, strangers buying him round after round, clapping him on his good shoulder and bragging of their own exploits on the vast waters of Lake Dorr or the Eastern Sea where Mangrove the City loomed over it on pale, marble cliffs and walls. His belly filled time and again with beer and he had to keep walking out the back door to empty his bladder in the alleyway that itself seemed to be flowing with a river of urine.

It was while there, standing in that dark, awful-smelling way, his pants down around his thighs, his dick in his good hand, that the blow fell. The club—wood padded with leather strips—thumped solidly against his skull and the next thing Hoggman knew was... well, nothing.

"Ugh," he heard himself say.

Hoggman's eyes hurt. They hurt terribly. He lifted his hand to ward off the glare that was burning down on his face and slowly, carefully, he peeled his sleep-glued eyes open until he could see.

"Oh," he said, drawing the lone syllable out until he figured that he should stop or end it by puking out the contents of his guts. So he just lay there for a while, covering his eyes with his hand. At least the gentle rocking made him feel better, as if he might not puke. At least just now.

And it was then that he realized that he was on the water. In a panic, he forced himself to sit up. Then, quickly grasping the situation, he leaned over the side of the boat and finally did vomit.

"Yer awake at last," said the voice. "I was beginning to worry I'd landed far too hard a blow on that hard noggin of yours. Took two whacks, it did."

Opening his eyes, bracing himself, Hoggman took stock of the situation. He was on a small fishing boat. Nothing fancy; oars for two men, a single mast, a tiny cabin and a hold that could contain maybe five hundred pounds of fish or other cargo. And he looked up to see the man at the oars, pulling hard to take them out ever farther into the vastness of Lake Dorr. "I don't know you," Hoggman said.

"Nay," the man replied. "And I'm sorry to take you as I did, but no other would come out with me. I tried to hire a hand, but all were either already employed or on their own to take the bounty." As the man spoke, he continued to pull on the huge, oak oars. His arms were like corded iron, bare and tanned; his hands were callused, but whether from oars or from some other honest work Hoggman could not say. At his feet was a large bundle tied in tough green canvas from which emanated an unearthly awful stench.

Aboard the boat where he could plainly see were six good harpoons and lengths of cord. There were also hooks of iron, perfect for snagging something as large and as awful as a krang was supposed to be.

"As things look, I'm lucky I did hire no one else. I've never met a man who had successfully killed a krang. Nor even seen one!" His eyes went wide at that and Hoggman was suddenly afraid, as if he were in the presence of madness. The promise of gold could do that to a man.

And the bounty the princes of Mangrove were offering for the krang was great. That much gold could indeed inspire a man with madness. Weren't the docks already filled with people crazed to earn the money? Hoggman groaned and leaned over the side, vomiting yet again. Maybe he could just slide overboard and swim back to shore. One arm he had, but he could swim just fine with it, krang or none. Lifting his head, he peered out and saw nothing but water stretching away to every horizon in which he looked. Lake Dorr was a vast place, he'd heard, but had never realized it until then, for he'd never actually been out on it.

"We're two miles out," the man said. "I can tell you were thinking of jumping. Don't." He nodded toward the harpoons. Then he nodded toward the scabbard secured to the oarlocks to his right. The sword was the real deal, high quality steel Hoggman could tell from the bit that glinted between the hilt and scabbard. "I'm not by nature a fisherman, but I'm in need of real money and... well... how much do I need to know with you on my side?" He smiled and the grin seemed genuine.

"I'm sick," Hoggman said. Perhaps he could talk him into heading back to shore.

"Don't worry," the warrior said. "I'll give you a fair share of the bounty. My boat, my harpoons, my line. But I'll cut you in. You just do your part and help me take the creature," and he continued to smile, his teeth all white and good and in their places.

The man was young and strong and either very stupid or very naïve. Hoggman wasn't sure which. But he had to either ride this out or talk his way back to shore. He did not belong out on these waters. He lay back and wiped his mouth, trying to figure a scheme that would work. "What is your name?" He asked. If he could break the ice he could talk his way out of the trouble.

"Danilov," the youth told him. "I'm a mercenary from the outlands, not far from the northern borders. But there's no one to fight these days. Mangrove's kings have crushed so many enemies that everyone's afraid of them. So." He looked down the length of the boat at Hoggman. "My family needs money and until I can take up my job as a free soldier again I have to find something else. This bounty. I'll kill the krang and... well, hell... it's enough to retire. I could grow old on that much gold!"

Rising, Hoggman tried to find his legs. The boat rolled and he rolled with it and almost fell. "There are five hundred... no, a thousand others trying to find the krang," he blurted. "We don't have a chance in Hell of finding that creature."

But the soldier smiled again. "My mother did not raise a fool," he insisted, pulling at those oars, taking the craft farther and farther into the huge lake. The wind was mild on them, the sun bright, the temperature even. It was as if they were out for a pleasant jaunt over the rolling waves of the lake. "I learned what it is that krang most desire. With the bait that I have brought, they cannot resist."

And then Hoggman once again eyed the canvas bundle at Danilov's feet. "But you should already know this. For you yourself have killed and caught a mighty krang!" That goddamned smile. Hoggman wondered about his odds of just picking up something and bludgeoning the fool and being done with it.

But then he watched the bunching and flexing of those amazing arms, saw the quick twitch of the youth's every move, and he knew that if he made the wrong choice his life was no good. He would just have to wait it out. That was all there was to it. How bad could it be? How long could they go?

After a while, Danilov stopped rowing. He stored the oars and stood on the platform aft and peered out into the lake.

"Good," he said, barely above a whisper. "We're alone." Indeed, there were no sails visible at all. There were no other boats anywhere—it was as if they had the lake to themselves. Danilov looked back toward Hoggman who was sitting in the lip of the small cabin, having stolen a glance now and then inside to note that the space there held casks of water and of wine and hard tack and dried beef. There was even a bed in there.

"We troll now," the soldier said.

"What?" Hoggman asked.

"We troll the lake. I have it on good authority that the krang will not be able to resist. It will be ours." The dark-headed man, his locks hanging down past his own shoulders spread those godlike arms. "And then the bounty will be ours! Yes?"

"Yes," Hoggman agreed. "Just as you say."

"Time to bait the hooks," the youth said. At that, he bent and began to untie the canvas bundle on the narrow deck. The beggar watched as the other man worked at the tight twine holding the baggage closed. As the fabric loosened, the stench from the canvas increased and became more sickening until, finally, the contents were visible. Inside the bag were parts of a person. And not just a person, but...

"They're so small," Hoggman croaked.

Danilov's eyes speared his shipmate. "I came by them honestly," he said. "I am not a killer of children," he insisted.

And yet again Hoggman went to the side of the boat so that he could vomit.

"You are a strange man for one who has killed the krang," the mercenary stated. "Now, help me bait the hooks."

***

All the day they fished the waters. Danilov had four hooks in the waters of Lake Dorr, each baited with the bits and pieces of the corpse of the child. Hoggman was afraid to ask him how he'd acquired those small limbs, and was only glad that all he had to do was sling the hooks overboard, tossing the awful hooks and their baits away from him.

The sun climbed into the sky. Hoggman learned all about how Danilov had hired his sword arm out to a dozen different dukedoms around the northern fringes of the nation of Mangrove. Unlike his own stories, these rang true, and as he listened to them he realized that he would be not just a fool to try to overpower the man, but also a dead fool. Between hearing tales of how the youth had hacked this man to bits or that soldier in half, Hoggman lied as best he could whenever Danilov asked him what they would go about the deed when it came time to do in the krang.

For his part, Hoggman could only hope that he'd been fed a line of bullocks concerning the attraction of krangs to the rotting bits of dead children.

"I was wondering," Danilov finally asked him, after they'd shared a biscuit and some water. "What exactly does a krang look like?"

Hoggman cleared his throat. He'd never seen one of those books the priests kept with pictures of them. And he'd never spoken to anyone who admitted to having seen one. The existence of the krang was just one of those things one accepted as true. After all, the princes themselves were so worried about them that they'd put up a ransom in reward for its capture and death.

"They're huge," Hoggman began. "Thirty feet from nose to tail. And armored like a rhino," he said. When Danilov nodded, he knew that he didn't have to elaborate on what a rhino was. "They have a mouth wide enough to bite a man in half. Or swallow him whole. And a row of teeth down each jaw like butcher knives. But white, like bone!"

"What color are they?" The soldier continued to pull at the oars, the lines and hooks trailing behind the boat.

"Well... they're like a fish," he said. "Green above and white on the belly. But with spots. Red spots."

He could tell that Danilov was going to ask him about the spots when suddenly one of the lines went taut. Then the boat actually turned in the direction of the line and began to list.

"I knew it," Danilov exclaimed. "The old witch never has steered me wrong!"

I'll be damned, Hoggman was thinking. His eyes bugged as the roped went suddenly deep and the boat tilted down, as if it might capsize. But before that could happen, the cord suddenly went slack and the boat righted itself.

"Damn," the soldier said. He began to reel in the line until the end came into his hands. The bait was gone, but the end of the thick iron hook was still on the cord; it had been bitten clean through, good iron though it was.

As Hoggman was sighing in relief that the hook had saved them, the boat was jerked from the other side, another line having been taken.

"Grab a harpoon," Danilov ordered his mate. "We'll gaff him when he comes to the surface." For that was precisely what

Hoggman had told him one had to do when the krang was brought to heel.

As the beggar grabbed up the weapon the tension on the new line went slack just as the previous one. And when the soldier reeled it in the hook was, like the other, bitten right through, as if it had been a bit of bread given to a diner in a tavern.

"We have two more hooks," the soldier told Hoggman. "We'll get him. If he takes the hook right he won't be able to slip it! We'll pull him in and nail him with our harpoons!" No sooner had these words left his mouth than the third hook was taken. Apparently the flesh of children was totally irresistible to whatever was beneath these waves.

This time, the tension in the line did not give and as Danilov pulled on the cord the beast below pulled back and the boat began to ride, the pair finding themselves careening through the low waves, spray flying, "This time," the soldier said.

But, as suddenly as it had begun, the sleigh ride ended. The boat settled down in the sea and they stared at the cord as Danilov pulled it in, still with the hook, but absent of the bait. "It took the others," he said, hope on his young face. "It must certainly take the remaining bait. Yes?"

Hoggman nodded, hoping he was wrong. "Yes. It certainly must."

But they waited. Nothing happened. No tension came on that last line and it did not move at all as the time slipped past them, the sun crawling across the sky to mark the day. "Maybe it fled," Hoggman told the other man, his eyes flicking back in the direction where he thought the shore might be.

"Oh, no," Danilov suddenly blurted. "What if..." And then he ran to that last baited line and began to pull it aboard, coiling the rope at his feet as he dragged at it. Finally, when he had it on the deck it was revealed as just the empty iron. He could see where the teeth had scraped along the metal, leaving the hook but having taken the bait.

The huge youth sat down on the deck and stared with great disappointment at the empty hook. His eyes swept out on the vast lake. Hoggman's own gaze followed that of the man who'd kidnapped him and there, no more than forty feet off the bow the krang came to the surface and rolled on its side, showing them one great eye that stared at them as if in challenge.

In fact, the krang looked nothing like Hoggman had described. It was not green with spots, but solid red, the color of arterial blood that Danilov had often seen gushing from men he'd cut down in battle. And its snout was nothing like that of a fish, but more like the bears he'd seen in the cold hills beyond the northern borders. And it had whiskers, not scales. It wasn't anything like the monster that Hoggman had delineated.

"I'm out of bait," Danilov said.

Hoggman cringed, realizing that the other's eyes were on him and not on the spot where the great krang had just slipped below the water. "We can go back," Hoggman said. "You can get more... more of that bait."

"No," the soldier said. "I never go back. I only go forward. That's the most important lesson of all. Only go forward." He said this as he reached down and plucked his sword from its spot along the oarlock. And just as Hoggman had suspected, it was revealed as most excellent steel when the mercenary drew it slowly out of its scabbard. "I see what I need and what I need is bait." His sword flashed in a precise arc and Hoggman saw that, indeed, he'd have been stupid to have challenged the youth.

***

These days one can see the man when he comes down to the docks to enjoy the inns where the beer flows, where he can tell his stories. Some say that he was once a beggar but now dresses in fine clothes and lives in a stout house in a fine part of Mangrove itself.

Sometimes, when he's in a good spirit, he will tell how he came by the cash that made him comfortable, if not rich. "I killed a krang," he'll say, sometimes even mentioning the glorious youth who had actually fought the animal and struck in the mortal blow. Then he'll tell how they're not really fish, but more like seals or whales, but vicious and foul and quick. He'll tell how they love to eat the flesh of children and how they can wipe out all of the fish in any place, even in an inland sea like Lake Dorr.

And often, when people hear his tale or laugh at his jokes, even though he is a rich man of means, they will buy him wine or mead and cheer him on as he speaks. Some will do this because he's just good old Hoggman who is full of piss and vinegar.

But some buy him a cup because he has but one arm.

TERNSKULL POINT

Matthew Fryer

Hallbjörn stepped out onto the frosted balcony of the lighthouse and jumped, almost dropping his coffee.

"Good grief."

The fjord teemed with walruses. They basked on the sheets of ice, slipping sinuously through the currents, their tusks gleaming bone-white beneath the moon. Several had clambered upon the narrow stack of Ternskull Point itself, heaped against the base of the lighthouse tower. The arctic midnight was alive with the sound of their eerie whistles and barks.

Hallbjörn took a deep breath and set his steaming mug down on the balcony railing. Their number had been growing steadily for the last couple of weeks, but had surely doubled since yesterday. At least.

A couple of cinnamon-coloured bulls were fighting on a nearby floe, the clatter of their tusks echoing across the black water of the fjord. At least twenty or so were heaped on the zig-zagging steps of the dock below, and the frost-burned wood bowed beneath the weight. Some even sprawled on the deck of the Snædís - Hallbjörn's small, reinforced trawler - and were rummaging through the coils of rope for stray gobbets of fish.

Hallbjörn leaned inside the balcony door. "Kristin?" he called down the curling staircase.

"What?"

"I think we have a problem!"

"Are you getting freaked out by the walruses again?"

"No!" Hallbjörn frowned indignantly. "Well, yes, but not without good reason. It's starting to look like a sealife sanctuary! Come and have a look!"

Hallbjörn made eye contact with a hulking alpha-male. It might have been his fearful imagination, but there seemed to be attitude in the bull's poise, an almost baleful look in its eyes. Although walruses didn't normally attack humans unless provoked, they could be aggressively territorial, and had apparently decided that they wanted Ternskull Point for their own.

Kristin appeared through the door, huddling against the cold. She blinked. "Wow. You weren't exaggerating."

"Why are we suddenly so interesting?"

Kristin shrugged, but Hallbjörn caught guilt behind her nonchalance. "Do you know something I don't?"

She shook her head and forced a smile. "Of course not. Have they caused any damage?"

"The dock's not going to last much longer. And there was one inside the Snædís cabin this afternoon. It'd smashed open the door, broken the seat and torn up my map books. I had to scare it off with the air-horn."

"They must be hungry," Kristin said. "Fish stocks are low this year,
and they associate boats with food."

"They're lucky I'm out of rounds for my shotgun, or they'd be associating boats with a faceful of buckshot."

"That's a little extreme."

"I don't think so. They can set up a new colony on some other poor bugger's doorstep."

"They're just walruses, Hallbjörn."

"Just walruses, indeed!" He shivered, the arctic breeze slicing through his jacket. "Try saying that when you're standing in front of a furious, two-ton bull!"

While they had always been a common sight around the fjords of eastern Greenland, Ternskull Point had never been invaded before, and Hallbjörn felt fiercely defensive of their home. The small island rose from the water like a lone, towering crag, its dappled flanks encrusted with permafrost and barnacles. With the lighthouse on top, it reminded Hallbjörn of a castle keep, which had probably exacerbated his warrior guardian spirit. And while the walruses had more right to be here than him – the coastline was their natural domain after all – he'd put far too much effort into making the lighthouse a snug little nest for Kristin and himself, and wasn't going to watch as it was slowly trashed.

His wife pursed her lips, and Hallbjörn again detected subterfuge in her manner. "They're probably just refugees from the glacial flood," she said.

That could well be true. Last month, a colossal meltwater lake - dammed in behind the coastal glaciers to the north - had burst its banks. The deluge had put Niagra Falls to shame, and scattered a busy colony there into the ocean.

Hallbjörn started as a guttural bellow burst up from the darkness. A couple of bulls were locked together, slamming against the wall of the lighthouse. Another nearby decided to join in, and lumbered towards the melee, bashing against the wooden handrail of the dock which broke off and tumbled into the sea.

"Oi!" Hallbjörn yelled.

"Calm down. You'll give yourself a coronary!"

"But this is our home! And how am I supposed to go down there and mend it?"

One of the bulls looked up and cocked its head, as though daring him to even try.

"You've got your air-horn. That does the trick."

"For now, maybe. But I swear that one in the Snædís was this close to charging me anyway."

"They only attack if threatened."

"Or hungry. Just look at them! You can see it in their eyes. They want
blood."

"Don't be so melodramatic." Kristin paused, then nodded out into the fjord. "Here comes another berg."

A small iceberg appeared from the darkness, crackling through the floes as though they were made of polystyrene: more scree from the northern glaciers. Since the meltwater flood, they'd gradually been shedding much of their fractured bulk. Hallbjörn had seen several ghostly sculptures gliding past the fjord, and trips out in the Snædís had become precarious to say the least. The local geophysics station, by which his wife was employed, did a lot of research into climate change and while Hallbjörn was no scientist, the consequences seemed pretty damned obvious to him.

This iceberg was about the size of a house and sparkled in the darkness, a crazy sculpture of shelves, arches and cave mouths. Walruses lounged on the lower ridges, peering up at the lighthouse with their bleak, amoral gaze.

Hallbjörn swallowed. The iceberg was heading straight towards the dock, and even seemed to be picking up speed in the shallow swell. The Snædís wouldn't stand a chance.

"Oh great. Just what we need."

"It's okay," Kristin said. "The current's got it."

She was mercifully correct: the iceberg had begun to turn in the water. Hallbjörn held his breath as it missed the dock by a whisker and glanced the side of the point. His coffee mug slipped from the railing, plummeted down and smashed on a bull's head, eliciting a cry of surprised anger from the enormous creature. Hallbjörn laughed, but his amusement soon vanished as the lights inside the lighthouse flickered and the iceberg scraped by with the sound of a thousand shrieking harpies.

He winced. "I hope the point can take this."

If their lighthouse had been built upon solid rock, there would have been no cause for concern, but Ternskull Point was man-made. It was a caisson: effectively just a huge, bottomless box that had been sunk into the fjord in order to build the foundations of a bridge. Hallbjörn had always been interested in engineering, and had read that this particular caisson dated back to the 19th century. It was constructed from sheet iron and timber on the mainland, before being floated out around the soaring cliffs and lowered into the bedrock. Once sealed in place, the water trapped inside was pumped out, and the builders were lowered into the gloom to chip away at the ancient ice and stone.

The proposed bridge was never built. It was designed to span the narrow fjord, to bypass the long route around the mountainous mainland, but the project was abandoned shortly after the caisson was in place. The creeping ice had soon absorbed it into the frozen, timeless landscape.

The iceberg carved alongside, spraying frost and sparks into the sea, rattling the balcony beneath their feet. It could easily damage the hollow structure – almost two hundred years old and battered by the frigid elements - and condemn Ternskull Point and its lighthouse to a watery grave.

Hallbjörn exhaled as the iceberg issued a final, Jurassic groan before the relative calm of the winter night returned.

Kristin sighed in relief. "That was close."

"Too close. Maybe moving out here wasn't such a good idea after all..."

His words faded as the stairs down to the dock started to collapse. Hallbjörn watched in horror as the wood splintered and groaned, walruses spilling into the icy water with heavy wet smacks. One of them fell onto the cabin of the Snædís with a resounding clang. The roof caved in like tinfoil and the cabin windows shattered.

Hallbjörn squeaked with impotent rage. "Brilliant! Now what the hell are we supposed to do?"

Kristin sighed. "Looks like we're really starting to see the consequences of the melt. In thirty years time, half the world will be underwater. Maybe then the climate change deniers will start to listen."

"We've got a problem that's a little more immediate!"

Hallbjörn peered over the railing at where the iceberg had ground against the caisson. Water was pouring out from inside, and several walruses rolled and turned beneath the cascade. "Oh, this just gets better. That berg's gouged a hole."

He frowned. This stuff wasn't pouring, it was slithering: a clotted, dark fluid with the consistency of cheap porridge. It wasn't just stagnant seawater, nor the detritus of dead marine life; it looked as though somebody had sliced open a bag of stew. The foam below darkened around the deluge, pushing back the chunks of ice, and beneath the light of the moon, Hallbjörn glimpsed grim shades of crimson.

"What is that?"

The reply that passed Kristin's lips was barely a croak.

"Corpses."

Hallbjörn gaped in realisation. The caisson was vomiting a flood of putrefying bodies into the sea. He glimpsed faces, shrunken torsos and entwined limbs in the blackened sludge, spreading around the base of the point. The oily splattering sound reminded him of a fishing trawler dumping its netted haul onto the deck, except that this just went on. And on.

The walruses began to gather around the hole, barking excitedly and plunging their bristled snouts into the quagmire.

"It's all true," Kristin said quietly.

The words jolted Hallbjörn from his reverie. "What?"

"I never thought... I'm so sorry. I should've told you."

"What are you talking about?" Hallbjörn demanded, his saliva suddenly thick. "There's a thousand dead bodies pouring out of our cellar, and you're telling me you knew about it?"

Kristin nodded, her mouth a thin white line.

"Well?"

"It was something Crazy Hugrún once told me. I didn't give it a second thought."

Hallbjörn's anger stalled. If that was the source of Kristin's information, he understood her dismissal. Crazy Hugrún was an alcoholic spinster who lived in an old fishing shack on the outskirts of Ternskull. She was basically harmless, and could usually be found propping up the town bar and regaling anybody who would listen with campfire yarns of ghosts and local myths that had no historical basis whatsoever.

"What did she tell you?"

"You know that in the 19th century, many of these arctic settlements were hit by a plague?"

"Of course. It was probably scrofula, and why the building of the fjord bridge was abandoned. Too many people died to..." Hallbjörn stopped as the pieces fell into place.

Kristin nodded. "Bodies were piling up, and the survivors worried that burying them in the ice, or even at sea, might spread the infection. Crazy Hugrún said they shipped them here, filled the caisson up, built the lighthouse on top and that was that."

Hallbjörn choked down a squirt of hot bile. The meaty splashing seemed to grow louder, expanding inside his skull.

"I'm sorry. But Crazy Hugrún was drunk as a Dutch whaler on shore leave, and I didn't believe a word, which is why I didn't mention it. You'd only have got upset."

His wife knew him well; Hallbjörn had a very thin skin when it came to the macabre, whether real or imagined. He twitched around places that had any kind of gruesome or haunted history, and avoided cemeteries with a singular determination. A visit to Auschwitz as a child had made him physically ill for a week. Even a Crazy Hugrún story about a mass grave beneath their home would've niggled. Now he knew it was true, it spun his head.

They had bought the decommissioned lighthouse six years ago, just after their wedding in the ruins of a Norse church down the coast. The local authority were glad to be rid of it, closing the sale for a pittance, and Hallbjörn had devoted much of his time renovating the old building.

It was isolated, but as Kristin worked as a marine researcher, she was in an ideal position to work from home. The day they moved in, Hallbjörn resigned from his job as Ternskull's harbourmaster. He helped with the practical side of Kristin's field trips, and took care of the lighthouse plumbing and electrics. He repaired weather and iceberg damage, and took the Snædís to the mainland for supplies. He'd even developed a talent for cooking with the redfish and polar cod he caught from the dock.

As Ternskull Point was so small, barely wider than the lighthouse itself, there were no residential outbuildings: their living accommodation was concentrated inside the tower. The ground floor housed their kitchen and storeroom. The first landing led into a low-ceilinged lounge that doubled as Kristin's study, and the second held the bathroom. The last floor, tucked away beneath the lantern room and balcony, was their cramped but cosy bedroom.

While it could be somewhat claustrophobic, they enjoyed each other's company, and only needed to step outside to experience the vast beauty of the natural world. The fjord was also a prime spot to enjoy the undulating green dance of the northern lights.

Hallbjörn had always found the idea of being a lighthouse keeper somewhat romantic. But not any more. The walrus invasion had already soured his vision, and after Kristin's revelation, the dream was stone dead.

"Hallbjörn? Are you okay?"

He prised his fists off the railing. "I'll be fine. This is just... I don't feel very well."

"I'm so sorry. I should've told you."

Down below, the flow of bodies was ebbing. Hallbjörn daren't even guess the number of dead, and there must be countless more still inside, packed beneath the level of the gash.

"At least it explains why they're here," Hallbjörn said, nodding towards the walruses that clustered in the emulsive tar, stringy flesh trailing from their tusks. "That's what you were thinking earlier on, isn't it."

"It crossed my mind," Kristin confessed. "The caisson must've finally started leaking its contents. The walruses must be ravenous to eat 200 year old carrion."

Hallbjörn licked his dry lips, wishing she hadn't said that. Walruses were approaching the point from all directions, drawn towards the sick banquet. "We'd better call someone."

Kristin nodded, tears dampening her cheeks. He'd never seen her look so cold and forlorn.

"I'm sorry for snapping at you. There's no reason why you should've believed Crazy Hugrún's ridiculous story."

The lighthouse jolted, flinging them both against the railing. The air thundered with the grind of masonry and a cloud of concrete dust billowed across the balcony. The lights inside stuttered, and went out.

The quiet returned almost as quickly as it had been shattered. Hallbjörn stood frozen to the spot, terrified of starting another quake. "I think it might be a good idea if we went downstairs. Right now."

"And do what?" Kristin whispered. "Jump in the sea? We wouldn't last ten seconds."

"We can launch the Snædís."

"What about the walruses?"

"Fuck them," Hallbjörn announced, enjoying the feel of that unprecedented cuss on his lips. His squeamish terror had evaporated, replaced by a furious bravado. "This is my home and my boat! And I'm taking them back!"

The lighthouse trembled, and a staccato series of industrial pops pierced the night.

"Let's go!" he yelled, but before they'd made it through the door, the ancient roof of the caisson caved in.

Hallbjörn's stomach slammed into the roof of his mouth as the entire lighthouse plunged into the depths of the caisson like a brick dropped into a half-empty bucket of sludge.

He didn't have time to brace himself for impact before the lighthouse landed in the soup, slamming them down against the balcony. The lantern above exploded like a shrapnel bomb, dashing them with shards of glass and Hallbjörn covered his head as hunks of ice rained down in the darkness.

The lighthouse lolled drunkenly to one side, bumped against the inner wall of the caisson, and fell still.

Hallbjörn opened his eyes. The caisson roof had completely collapsed and a couple of curious walruses peered down from the fractured lip, silhouetted against a black, starlit sky. Hallbjörn dragged himself across the sloping floor. "Kristin! Are you okay?"

"I... I think so." She reached out and clasped his hand. His body webbed with pain and he tasted blood, but nothing seemed to be broken.

The inner wall of the caisson loomed around them, rutted with outcrops of dirty ice. Hallbjörn helped his wife up and they peered down over the side of the creaking balcony.

Corpses filled the lower half of the caisson like an immense cauldron of bad gruel. The dead had been preserved by the sea salt and subzero temperatures to some degree, but the decay would not be denied, and the sickly-sweet smell fogged the air, greasing Hallbjörn's lungs. He clenched his jaw, staring at the mass of waterlogged limbs and gaunt faces, bones jutting from the jelly.

"Look," Kristin said, pointing into the depths.

There were walruses down there, lounging amongst the dead.

"Pity they didn't break their necks in the fall."

Kristin shook her head. "They were already here."

Hallbjörn saw what she meant. Their matted fur was deeply stained, eyes shining from the crimson carnage like slices of onyx. They looked truly demented, clots of blood dripping from fractured tusks. One of them tore a soggy loop of intestine from a corpse pinned beneath its flippers, choked it down, then looked up at Hallbjörn with naked, rancid lust.

He swayed, clutching the rail. "How did they get inside?"

"Before we moved in, the ice around the top of the caisson had plenty of nooks and crevices."

"But the authorities patched up the holes before they started trying to sell the lighthouse. And anyway, those bulls would need a gap the size of a barn door!"

"Not when they were calves."

The penny dropped, and Hallbjörn's bowels twisted cold. It took a walrus years to reach adult size. If they'd been confined to the festering darkness since they were curious babies, blind and poisoned by their diet, no wonder they were delirious. For a moment, he actually pitied them.

More stirred in the sunken shadows of the pit. They moved slowly, flippers slapping across the flesh pool as though drunk, bilious seawater drooling from their mouths. One of the larger bulls raised its head and slashed at another walrus nearby, shaving a fat sliver of blubber from the smaller creature's neck. The victim snarled, and the two sank into a boiling frenzy of blood, ripping and growling in their cradle of gnawed corpses.

It was a pure snapshot of hell.

"Maybe it's the plague meat that's sent them crazy?" Kristin whispered.

"If so, the colony outside won't be far behind them." From the night, came the gristly crackle of feasting. Hallbjörn shuddered, fearing a faint.

Kristin sagged in defeat. "Oh no."

"What?"

"We're going down."

She was right. The lighthouse was sinking into the corpses, a menacing gurgle rising from its guts. Hallbjörn heard soft pops as skulls burst against the walls, the wet sigh of organs rupturing, bubbling their gases up through the swamp.

The lighthouse rumbled against the caisson wall, bumping over the meltwater crags. Disembodied limbs and cadavers protruded from the outcrops of ice, dangling like obscene baubles.

Hallbjörn's gorge rose, but he willed his throat shut, cursing his constitution. He had a duty to protect his wife, and couldn't achieve that whilst honking all over the place like some stupid, seasick tourist. He took a deep breath.

"I reckon we could climb up here and get out."

Kristin blinked. "Are you serious?"

"The only other option is that." Hallbjörn pointed down at the hole the iceberg had earlier torn in the caisson wall. Displacement caused by the lighthouse had resumed the flow of bodies out into the night. "Like you said, we wouldn't last ten seconds in the water. And that's if we got past the walruses!"

The bull he'd regarded earlier lifted its head and barked, the sound ricocheting around the caisson like the chime of a flat bell. It was a sound of confusion, pain and pure rage.

Kristin's face had gone chalk white. "Okay."

"Wait here," Hallbjörn said as the sludge reached the kitchen windows of the ground floor and began to pour inside, meat snagging on the broken glass.

Kristin grabbed his hand. "Where are you going?"

"My climbing gear's down in the storeroom. We'll need it to scale the ice."

"But the kitchen's already below..."

"I know! There's no time!" Hallbjörn shook his hand free. "Stay there!"

He hurried inside and took the skewed stairs four at a time, almost losing his footing. It plunged darker as he spiralled, lit only by the pallid moonlight that trickled through the windows, and by the time he reached the open-plan kitchen, he could barely see a thing. His boots sank into a curdled fluid that clung to his ankles like albumen. He could just make out the flayed torsos and limbs that had slithered inside, forming drifts beneath the windows, but they'd soon become clogged and reduced the flood of sickness to a drool. One of the walruses had squeezed its head through, but thankfully the window was too small for its bulbous body. It sniffed at the fetid air, bloody bristles quivering in the murk.

The front door groaned, bulging inwards beneath the pressure. A pair of tusks punched through the wood.

Hallbjörn's heart trip-hammered as he rushed into the storeroom. Silently thanking God that he was so organised around the house, he quickly located his pickaxe and crampons.

"Hallbjörn!" Kristin wailed from above. "We're sinking faster! Hurry up!"

Clutching his equipment, he waded from the store, fluid sucking at calves. Cracks spidered across the walls, and as he reached the foot of the staircase, the front door burst open. The semiliquid spewed inside, a walrus surfing the infected swell.

Hallbjörn bolted up the steps but slipped, windmilling cartoonishly, sending his pickaxe and crampons up into the air.

He managed to draw breath just before he fell back and plunged into the gore. It engulfed him completely, bitter cold shocking his body. The world went quiet. Heart booming in the silence, Hallbjörn tasted rotten blood, bile and salt, the flavours slamming through his senses. He burst up and squealed, pawing his face and slapping at the corpses that rolled lasciviously around his waist.

He flailed to his feet and saw that the intruding walrus had got its head wedged inside a rotting ribcage. The beast growled, bashing its head against the wall to dislodge it, and Hallbjörn seized the distraction. He hurried back onto the stairs, delving in the lumpy shallows for his gear. He quickly found the pickaxe, then grasped what he thought was one of the crampons. Dull moonlight fell upon the crumbling pelvis of a child. Hallbjörn dropped it and vomited down the front of his sodden jacket.

The walrus bayed. It had smashed the ribcage off, and was lumbering through the mulch, rheumy gaze upon him. Forsaking the search, Hallbjörn scrabbled up the staircase. Tusks scraped mockingly at the concrete in his wake.

Slipping on the slime, Hallbjörn tore up the circling stairs without looking back and after several painful tumbles, finally burst back on to the balcony. The open sky looked much further away already.

Kristin paled, taking in the unspeakable mucous that swung in thin ropes from his body. "Oh God..."

"I'm okay," he lied transparently, brandishing the pickaxe. "You hang on to me, and I'll grip one of these ridges. We're still fairly close to the top, we should be able to make our way up."

A wide ridge of blood-flecked ice was just drawing level with the descending balcony. Hallbjörn glanced back at Kristin, opening his mouth to speak, but something made him look up.

A walrus hunched on the rim of the broken lantern.

This bull was fresh and clean, unlike the disease-fed monstrosity that was squeezing its way upstairs. It must have jumped down from the lip of the caisson.

Hallbjörn stepped in front of his wife, raising the pickaxe. "Back off!"

The bloated creature could probably squash them both flat with a single belly-flop. It barked once, the sharp sound ringing through Hallbjörn's teeth. Then it lunged.

Hallbjörn swung his weapon but his arm smacked against a solid flipper, the pickaxe barely making contact. A tusk smashed into the side of his head and rattled his brain. He saw stars, but managed to swing the pickaxe again and it punched into the walrus's flank. He wasn't sure how deep it cut through the blubber, but the wound was enough to make his attacker roar. It slithered forward from the lantern and crashed down on to the balcony, almost ripping the construction from the lighthouse wall. Hallbjörn stumbled back and kicked out, his boot connecting with its snout, but lost his balance and fell into the damaged railing. It gave way and he dropped the pickaxe in panic, grasping at thin air.

"Hallbjörn!" Kristin screamed as he tumbled over the edge.

His stomach soared for a second before he punched head-first into the sickening pool like a fat dart, immersed to his waist. His legs whiplashed, arcs of pain fanning from his spine.

He screwed up his eyes and mouth as he tried to thrash free, cringing in unbearable anticipation at the thought of tusks stabbing into his unprotected legs and genitals. Finally wrenching his torso from the soup, he gagged, clawing at the cheese-like flesh smeared into his eyes.

Several bulls lurched through the pool towards him, crushing faces and snapping brittle limbs in their vigour.

"No!" Kristin's voice, shrill with dread.

Hallbjörn squinted up, the top of the sinking lighthouse only about fifteen feet above him now. The walrus reared and knocked Kristin to the balcony floor, then leapt upon her like some kind of obese rapist, its tusks hacking at her neck and breasts.

"Get your filthy flippers off my wife!" Hallbjörn yelled, trying to haul himself through the corpses, oblivious to the horror and the agony in his bruised back, snatching handfuls of frozen meat. But the harder he fought, the more snagged he became.

He looked up just in time to see the bull flip Kristin over the railing. She spun down and landed face-up beside him with a splat, splashing his face with seawater and stagnant gore.

"Kristin!"

She keened like a seal pup and feebly tried to sit up. Hallbjörn leaned forward and pressed his hand to the steaming punctures around her throat. Her blood felt flame-hot against his numb skin. "You're going to be okay. I love you, Kristin. And I'm going to get you out of here."

"I know." She sobbed weakly. "And I love...."

The shadow of a bull fell across them just a moment before its tusks plunged down into Kristin's eye sockets with a jellied crunch, thudding into the back of her skull.

Hallbjörn gaped as the crimson behemoth raised its head, lifting Kristin's body like a prize. Her body dangled, twitching, still impaled on its tusks as the bull towered above him. It bellowed, rippling with deranged strength, and Kristin's head slipped free with a wet snick. Her lifeless corpse splashed back down into the swamp. Hallbjörn stared at the deep, black wounds of her eyes. His bladder relaxed, strength melting from his muscles. He giggled: an ugly, broken sound.

The carcasses nuzzled him, bones scratching at his skin as he began to drift away from his wife and her hulking slayer. He was caught in the languid current, being carried towards the hole in the caisson wall.

More bulls advanced from the gloom. Beyond them, the lighthouse sank rapidly, and finally disappeared beneath the surface with a prolonged, reverberating belch.

"You want Ternskull Point?" he mumbled. "You're welcome to it."

Hallbjörn slithered out through the hole and glimpsed countless eyes and reddened tusks, waiting in the icy water of the fjord below.

As Kristin had said, he wouldn't last ten seconds.

He hoped not, anyway.

THE END

DEAD BAIT 2 AUTHORS

James Robert Smith has sold more than sixty short stories during his writing career. He has also had comic scripts published by Kitchen Sink, Spyderbabies Grafix, Marvel Comics, and others. His eco-thriller THE FLOCK was published in 2010 by Tor-Forge Books in the US. Its sequel, THE CLAN, will follow in late 2011. The movie rights to THE FLOCK were acquired by producers Don Murphy (TRANSFORMERS, NATURAL BORN KILLERS) and John Wells (ER, West Wing). His zombie novel THE LIVING END: A Zombie Novel (with Dogs) is forthcoming from Severed Press. Smith lives in the state of North Carolina with his wife, Carole, and three cats. They have one adult son (Andrew).
www.jamesrobertsmith.net

A native of Philadelphia, NY Timesand best-selling international author **Steve Alten** earned his Bachelor's degree from Penn State University, his Masters from the University of Delaware, and his Doctorate from Temple University. He is the author of the Meg series, Domain series, Goliath, The Loch, and The Shell Game. Steve Alten is also founder and director of Adopt-An-Author, a free nationwide teen reading program that is now being used in thousands of secondary school classrooms across the country to excite reluctant readers to read. For more information go to www.AdoptAnAuthor.com and www.SteveAlten.com

James Harris is a writer residing in Sussex, UK, the only place he feels comfortable. He shares a house with his wife and two eerily intelligent cats. His publishing credits include: Withersin Magazine, The Willows Magazine, The Great Suspense & Mystery Magazine, The British Fantasy Society

Journal, Severed Press: Dead Bait 1 & 2, and Read Raw Press: Raw Terror Anthology.

Cody Goodfellow has written three solo novels—Radiant Dawn, Ravenous Dusk and Perfect Union—and three more with John Skipp—Jake's Wake, The Day Before and Spore. His recent short fiction and comics have appeared in Black Static, Creepy, Strange Aeons, Cemetery Dance, Daikaiju, Mighty Unclean and Cthulhu Unbound 3. He enjoys boating, surfing and scuba diving because—not in spite of—the ocean's many and diabolical attempts to murder him.

Anthony Wedd was born in Ceduna in South Australia in 1971. He spent time in a variety of country towns across South Australia as a child before studying Physics at Flinders University in Adelaide. After brief stints as a computer programmer and an applied physicist, he became a meteorologist in 1999 and moved to Brisbane, where he still resides. He has been a devoted fan of the horror genre since adolescence, and has also appeared in *Zombie Zoology* from Severed Press. In his spare time, he enjoys writing and holidaying on the South Australian coast

Matthew Fryer was born and bred in Sheffield, England. He studied English at university, but now works in the windowless basement of his local hospital where he gets to wear blue pyjamas and play with machines that go bing!
He writes mainly horror and humorous fantasy, and his stories can be found in publications such as Space and Time, Dark Jesters, Necrotic Tissue and Andromeda Spaceways Inflight Magazine.
He lives with his wife, Allison, and spends too much of his time losing at poker, listening to loud music, and hoping it will rain so that he doesn't have to mow the lawn. They have a deranged cat that looks like Hitler.
Visit his website, the cheesily-titled Hellforge, at www.matthewfryer.com.

Michael Hodges is a speculative fiction writer who lives in Chicago, Illinois. He's currently revising two novels, and his short story "Revenge on Apex Mountain" is forthcoming in Fearology 2. He's an outdoor nut who enjoys fly fishing and camping, especially in the Northern Rocky Mountains. More information is available at his site, michaelhodgesfiction.com.

Murphy Edwards has appeared in over fifty professional magazines and journals including, Dimensions Magazine, The East Side Edition, Black October, Horizons, MidAtlantic Monthly, Modern Drummer, The Nor'Easter, Walking Bones, Escaping Elsewhere, Trail of Indiscretion, Hardboiled Magazine, Barbaric Yawp, Samsara, The Magazine of Suffering, The Nocturnal Lyric , Night Chills and in the anthologies Dead Bait , Assassin's Canon , Abaculus II and Night Terrors. His short story, "Mister Checkers", was chosen to be among the best in science fiction, fantasy and horror of 2009 for the Leucrota Press Anthology, Abaculus III. Edward's work to date includes excursions into horror, hard-boiled, thrillers, crime mysteries, westerns and contemporary fiction. He currently resides in Indiana.

Paul A. Freeman is the author of Rumours of Ophir, a novel set in Zimbabwe which is presently on that country's high school English literature syllabus. He writes largely crime and horror fiction, and his short stories have been widely published.
His narrative poem-novella, Robin Hood and Friar Tuck: Zombie Killers – A Canterbury Tale by Paul A. Freeman, was published in 2009 by Coscom Entertainment, and his crime novel, Vice and Virtue, set in Saudi Arabia, was published in 2010, in German translation, by Pulp Master.
Currently, he works in Abu Dhabi, where he lives with his wife and three children.
He can be found on line at www.paulfreeman.weebly.com

RALEIGH DUGAL writes fiction and non-fiction. He enjoys highways, football, and thunderstorms. He has a couple of degrees and knows how to juggle. His fiction has been published in Encounters Magazine and An Honest Lie, and his short story "Our Subterranean Complex" was nominated for a 2011 Pushcart Prize. He lives in Boston, Massachusetts.

The Oxford Companion to English Literature describes **Ramsey Campbell** as 'Britain's most respected living horror writer'. He has been awarded the Grand Master Award of the World Horror Convention and the Lifetime Achievement Award of the Horror Writers Association. His regular columns appear in All Hallows, Dead Reckonings and Video Watchdog. He is the President of the British Fantasy Society. **www.ramseycampbell.com**

Guy N Smith wrote his first horror book, Werewolf by Moonlight in 1974, which spawned two sequels. He is probably best known for a series of six Crabs books, the first of which, Night of the Crabs, was published in 1976. A prolific writer, Guy has had over a thousand short stories and magazine articles published. He has written a series of children's books under the pseudonym Jonathon Guy, two thrillers under the name Gavin Newman and a dozen non-fiction books on countryside matters. But, it is for his 70 or so horror books that he is best known. **www.guynsmith.com**

Tim Curran lives in Michigan and is the author of the novels Skin Medicine, Hive, Dead Sea, Resurrection, The Devil Next Door, and Biohazard. Upcoming projects include Graveworm from Severed Press and Bone Marrow Stew, a short story collection from Tasmaniac Publications. His short stories have appeared in such magazines as City Slab, Flesh&Blood, Book of Dark Wisdom, and Inhuman, as well as anthologies such as Dead Bait, Shivers IV, High Seas Cthulhu, and, Vile Things. Find him on the web at: www.corpseking.com

WHITE FLAG OF THE DEAD
Joseph Talluto

**Book 1
Surrender of
the Living.**

Millions died when the Enillo Virus swept the earth. Millions more were lost when the victims of the plague refused to stay dead, instead rising to slay and feed on those left alive. For survivors like John Talon and his son Jake, they are faced with a choice: Do they submit to the dead, raising the white flag of surrender? Or do they find the will to fight, to try and hang on to the last shreds or humanity?

Surrender of the Living is the first high octane instalment in the White Flag of the Dead series.

DEMONMACHY
Brant Danay

As the universe slowly dies, all demonkind is at war in a tournament of genocide. The prize? Nirvana. The Necrodelic, a death addict who smokes the flesh of his victims as a drug, is determined to win this afterlife for himself. His quest has taken him to the planet Grystiawa, and into a duel with a dream-devouring snake demon who is more than he seems. Grystiawa has also been chosen as the final battleground in the ancient spider-serpent wars. As armies of arachnid monstrosities and ophidian gladiators converge upon the planet, the Necrodelic is forced to choose sides in a cataclysmic combat that could well prove his demise. Beyond Grystiawa, a Siamese twin incubus and succubus, a brain-raping nightmare fetishist, a gargantuan insect queen, and an entire universe of genocidal demons are forming battle plans of their own. Observing the apocalyptic carnage all the while is Satan himself, watching voyeuristically from the very Hell in which all those who fail will be damned to eternal torment. Who will emerge victorious from this cosmic armageddon? And what awaits the victor beyond the blood-drenched end of time? The battle begins in Demonmachy. Twisting Satanic mythologies and Eastern religions into an ultraviolent grotesque nightmare, the Messiah of Death Saga will rip your eyeballs right out of your skull. Addicted to its psychedelic darkness, you'll immediately sew and screw and staple and weld them back into their sockets so you can read more. It's an intergalactic, interdimensional harrowing that you'll never forget...and may never recover from.

Available at www.severedpress.com, Amazon and most online bookstores

GREY DOGS
IAN SANDUSKY

WHEN GOD TURNS HIS BACK ON THE EARTH

Fires blaze out of control. Looters are run through with speeding lead. Children scream as their flesh is torn by broken teeth. Firearms insistently discharge in the night air. Over it all, the moans of the infected crowd out any pause for silence.

THE EPIDEMIC SHOWS NO MERCY

Men. Women. Fathers. Daughters. Wives. Brothers. All are susceptible, and the viral infection is a death sentence. One hundred percent communicable. One hundred percent untreatable. It's making people insane, turning them feral. *Zombies.* No end is in sight, and Carey Cardinal has run out of options.

ONE SHOT AT SEEING SUNRISE

Past lives, shadowed histories and long-kept secrets will emerge, making the twisted road ahead ever more difficult to navigate as Carey will discover a foe far more dangerous than the shattered grey dogs - himself.

The Official Zombie Handbook: Sean T Page

Since pre-history, the living dead have been among us, with documented outbreaks from ancient Babylon and Rome right up to the present day. But what if we were to suffer a zombie apocalypse in the UK today? Through meticulous research and field work, The Official Zombie Handbook (UK) is the only guide you need to make it through a major zombie outbreak in the UK, including: -Full analysis of the latest scientific information available on the zombie virus, the living dead creatures it creates and most importantly, how to take them down - UK style. Everything you need to implement a complete 90 Day Zombie Survival Plan for you and your family including home fortification, foraging for supplies and even surviving a ghoul siege. Detailed case studies and guidelines on how to battle the living dead, which weapons to use, where to hide out and how to survive in a country dominated by millions of bloodthirsty zombies. Packed with invaluable information, the genesis of this handbook was the realisation that our country is sleep walking towards a catastrophe - that is the day when an outbreak of zombies will reach critical mass and turn our green and pleasant land into a grey and shambling wasteland. Remember, don't become a cheap meat snack for the zombies!

BIOHAZARD

Tim Curran

The day after tomorrow: Nuclear fallout. Mutations. Deadly pandemics. Corpse wagons. Body pits. Empty cities. The human race trembling on the edge of extinction. Only the desperate survive. One of them is Rick Nash. But there is a price for survival: communion with a ravenous evil born from the furnace of radioactive waste. It demands sacrifice. Only it can keep Nash one step ahead of the nightmare that stalks him-a sentient, seething plague-entity that stalks its chosen prey: the last of the human race. To accept it is a living death. To defy it, a hell beyond imagining

THE LIVING END
James Robert Smith

One Hundred and Fifty Million Zombies.

Sixty Million Dogs.

All of them hungry for warm human flesh.

The dead have risen, killing anyone they find. The living know what's caused it-a vicious contagion. But too late to stop it. For now, what remains of society are busy shutting down nuclear reactors and securing chemical plants to prevent runaway reactions in both. There's little time for anything else.

Failed comic book artist Rick Nuttman and his family have joined thousands of other desperate people in trying to find a haven from the madness.

Perhaps refuge can be found in the village of Sparta or maybe there is salvation in The City of Ruth, a community raised from the ashes of Carolina.

In the low country below the hills, a monster named Danger Man changes everything.

While watching over it all, the mysterious figure of BC, moving his gigantic canine pack westward, into lands where survivors think they are safe

And always, the mindless hordes neither living nor dead, waiting only to destroy.

There will be a reckoning.

RINGLAND

8/11/8

Lightning Source UK Ltd.
Milton Keynes UK
UKOW04f0628141217
314454UK00001B/57/P

9 780980 606546